Another Way to Be

ANOTHER WAY TO BE

◆

The Path Within

Michael Hansen

HIGHPOINT EXPERIENCE

2005

Highpoint Experience
P. O. Box 384
Clinton, WA 98236

ISBN-13: 978-0-9765858-0-0
ISBN-10: 0-9765858-0-4

LCCN: 2005922357
First printing, June 2005
Printed in Canada on chlorine-free 100% recycled paper

10   9   8   7   6   5   4   3   2   1

To Carmen

ACKNOWLEDGEMENTS

◆

I HAVE BENEFITED from many gifted teachers, more than I am able to adequately convey. Some have been with me for decades and others I barely knew. They have been friends, colleagues, family members, adults, children, and one or two who were something other than human. I call them teachers because they planted seeds of awareness that have evolved within me. For those who may recognize the essence of a familiar seed, I am sincerely grateful for your contributions to this endeavor.

Specifically, I would like to extend my appreciation to Karen Cook, life partner and truth teller, for feedback, support, and a steadfast belief in my work. Thank you to Peggy Taylor, Celeste Mergens, and Darcy Pattison for guidance during a pivotal mid-course correction. Thanks also to Susan Osborn, Kurt Hoelting, Rick Ingrasci, and Julie Glover for open and honest feedback, and to Robert Kenny, Sally Goodwin, Charles Terry and Betsy MacGregor for creating a safe place to test my wings.

Special thanks to Tom Giffin for his magical artwork, Doug Hansen for his skillful design and layout, and Vivienne Hull for her detailed copy editing. Lastly, to my Mom and Dad for years of unwavering support and to Becker and Hanna for graciously allowing me the time and the space to write. A deep bow of gratitude to you all.

CONTENTS

◆

ANOTHER WAY TO BE

fa•ble (faˈbəl), n.1: a fictitious narrative that
illustrates a moral lesson or spiritual principle,
often with animals or inanimate objects
as characters; 2: an allegorical story that conveys
meaning indirectly by the use of comparison,
analogy, or metaphor; 3: a tale about supernatural
or extraordinary persons or incidents.

Olympia, Washington

1978

CROSSING PATHS

◆

THE MORNING SUN on my face was a welcomed relief after two weeks of nearly constant drizzle. Students were gathered in small groups soaking up the warmth as I strolled through Red Square, the expansive brick courtyard in the middle of campus. A melodic birdcall drew my attention to a row of sycamore trees. I paused and scanned the nearby branches. Nothing.

Beneath the budding limbs, a pair of sturdy benches were anchored firmly to the ground. On the bench nearest me sat a man; head tilted forward, palms pressed together, fingertips touching his lips. Filtered sunlight illuminated his short salt and pepper hair. It took me a moment to realize that it was man, not bird, producing the enchanting sound. His hands parted the instant our eyes met. He blinked – slowly, one time – before speaking.

1

"We are not human beings having a spiritual experience, we are spiritual beings having a human experience."

His words resonated in my belly like the sound of a gong. I turned without thinking, walked towards him, and asked in a voice that did not sound completely like my own, "What did you say?"

His lean supple body rose in a single fluid motion, halting my approach. The intensity of his gaze penetrated my body, mind, and spirit with the most powerful stillness I had ever experienced. Something inside of me let go and I slid into a dimension that had no clear reference points. Confusion gave way to fear as I attempted to orient myself in the unfamiliar landscape. Then, in the distance, a voice. The slow vibration of the words washed over me, pulling me back from wherever I had been.

"We are spiritual beings having a human experience..."

I found myself staring into the liquid eyes of a weathered face that was staring back at me. My mind was jumbled and yet I felt a strange sense of calm as I began to organize my thoughts into something that resembled a familiar order.

"My name is José Humevo." His enunciation was clear and concise: *hoe-`say hew-`may-vo*. His eyes scanned my body as he gave me a vigorous handshake.

It took me a moment to respond. "Nils Christiansen."

He released my hand and softened his gaze. "Human consciousness is not as fixed as it appears to be, it is much more pliable than most people imagine. Awareness is what we experience. It is not who we are." He nodded his head and turned to walk away. Looking back he added, "It was a pleasure to have crossed your path."

He disappeared into a crowd of students mingling in the courtyard, leaving me with a dazed look on my face and a pile of questions at my feet. I stood next to the empty bench, motionless. A ray of sunlight caught the corner of my eye and jolted me back into my body. I looked at my watch. I was late for class.

I hated to be late for anything. It rubbed against my Scandinavian values of order and control. My encounter with José Humevo had challenged those values and stirred up equal parts of fear and fascination within me. His words had poked a hole in the thin facade of my well-organized universe and caused me to question – everything. I could not shake the memory of his gaze. It was as if he had seen right through me.

When I saw José Humevo again he was sitting on that same bench, looking in my direction. Three days had passed. It was an overcast morning. There were butterflies in my stomach as I approached him. He moved to a standing position seemingly without effort and smiled at me with a boyish grin that somehow matched the rest of his well-worn face.

"Let's take a walk."

We crossed Red Square in silence and made our way to a grassy meadow behind the library. From there we entered the trailhead of a path that meandered through the forest and led to Eld Inlet, a thin finger of salt water on the

3

southern tip of Puget Sound. This access to forest and beach was a pivotal factor in my decision to come to the Evergreen State College. I felt at home in nature and walking on the trail that morning eased the tension that had been stirring in my belly.

The familiar tap-tap-tap of beak on wood pulled my attention away from the trail. I spotted the flaming red crest and staccato movement of a pileated woodpecker chopping away at a large western red cedar, wood chips flying over his surprisingly broad shoulders. He took flight and followed us, darting from tree to tree, as we passed through his territory.

I could not remember any of the questions I had been gathering to ask José Humevo. His quiet strength oozed into my awareness and brought me fully present to the moment. A hint of salt air wafted through the forest. It reached my nose the instant he began to speak.

"I am a learning guide. I have attained a certain level of understanding and knowledge about the nature of human awareness. I am not a student of any specific spiritual tradition. The things I know have simply come to me over time. It would be more accurate to say that they are continuing to come to me. It is an on-going journey."

The sound of his voice hung in the air for a single heartbeat, allowing my mind to catch up with his words.

"There are two portals between Human Beings and the Universe, or what I refer to as me and *not me*. One portal is an intake; it allows energy, life force, and chi to enter into my life. The other portal is an outlet; it allows energy, life force, and chi to flow out of my life. The degree to which either one of these portals is open or closed determines the level at which this universal energy is able to flow through me.

"It is a very simple concept that most people simply haven't taken the time to look at. Some people give and give and give but do not know how to receive. Others focus on getting, or having, or keeping, but do not know how to share what they acquire. Neither of these patterns is very effective. The former creates a constriction in the intake portal and the latter creates a constriction in the outlet portal. In either case the energy flow is constricted or cut off all together and life is experienced as difficult, challenging, meaningless.

"The solution to this problem is quite simple; figure out which portal is not as open as it could be and allow it to relax and open further. The experience of allowing the universal stream of infinite and eternal abundance to flow freely into and out of one's life is the most natural thing there is. At our core we all know how to do this, once we get out of our own way. Access to this abundance is our birthright.

"I have been blessed with a large and relaxed intake portal; abundance flows quite freely into my life. It is on the outlet side where I still have work to do. I am so full of abundance at this moment that there is no room for more to enter. It is time for me, once again, to increase the size of my outlet portal.

"The place where I am most aware of not allowing abundance to flow is around sharing my *principles of learning*. As far as I can tell, these principles are in alignment with the universal flow of abundance, but somewhat out of sync with current human understanding. I have a concern that my concepts will not be well received at this time."

José Humevo stopped walking. He turned and looked me in the eye.

"Actually, It's more than a concern, it's a fear."

He paused for a moment and glanced sideways.

"I have an acronym for the word *fear* – Fantasized Experience Appearing Real. Maybe my concepts will be misunderstood and maybe they won't. There is only one way to find out. Either I run my fears or my fears run me. This is the first *principle of learning*.

"The moment I face that which I fear, it begins to lose its power. I spent years avoiding, running from, or resisting my fears before I discovered this secret. Some fears are more persistent than others, but the principle works every time as long as I stay with it.

"I saw an opportunity when you crossed my path the other day. Your intake portal was open and relaxed, a good match for what I wanted to share. I dangled a hook in front of you and you took the bait, just like that."

He snapped his fingers and smiled. I began to ask a question, but he held up his hand to stop me.

"If you are interested, I will share the *principles of learning* that I am developing. First, let me say that all of this needs to be handled lightly. The information I have to share has nothing to do with ego gratification or spiritual snobbery, other than to remind us that taking anything too seriously is the one thing that will always trip us up.

Humor and humility are stepping stones along the way. This is the second *principle of learning*. We are all Bozos on this bus and people who think they are not, are only fooling themselves."

José Humevo chuckled to himself. It was a free-spirited laugh that filled me with a sense of well being. He started walking. I followed close behind.

"I am not more or less special than anyone else, and neither are you. Each and every one of us is completely unique and utterly common. Like the fingers of the hand, we cannot escape our uniqueness or our commonality. We are the same and we are different, all at the same time, all in our own way. Human awareness is a paradox that twists and turns and flips back on itself over and over again. I am offering to guide you through this terrain and in the process of guiding you I will also guide myself.

"We live in a world filled with a level of magic, awe, and mystery that most of us have lost sight of. Somewhere along the way humanity wandered off the path and we have been stumbling around in the forest, fearing life, fearing death, protecting ourselves from all that is *not me*.

"This is the greatest waste of time I can think of. We live in an abundant universe and we squander that abundance, individually and collectively, day after day. To be fully human requires that we embrace life with humor and humility. The universe is not out to get us. It is trying to *get us out* – out of our limited thinking, our limited feeling, our limited believing. It is attempting to guide us back to the path of awareness, understanding, and knowledge that we wandered away from so long ago we have forgotten it ever existed at all. The path does exist, it always has and it always will. It is right under our feet, available to all, as soon as we have eyes to see."

The forest trail opened to the expansiveness of the Eld Inlet. A gentle breeze blew across the water. José Humevo sniffed the air and looked up and down the beach before proceeding. I followed him to a large silvery-white driftwood log. He sat down and patted the sand beside him, looked at me, and cocked his head.

We leaned against the weathered log without speaking, eyes forward. I felt the pulse of the waves against the shore. The rhythm was effortless. There was no struggle here, no fighting for power, no need to control. It was a dance between water and earth, a place where two worlds touched. The sensation of openness and ease was simultaneously euphoric and disorienting. Once again, the questions that had been forming in my mind simply dropped away. My body rocked back and forth to the beat of the waves. There was something stirring within me that I could not name. I closed my eyes for a moment, and then there was nothing.

———————

It was black, the blackest black I had ever known. No movement, no sound, no smell. Then, a glimmer in the distance. I struggled to move forward. It felt like I was running through molasses. The glimmer shifted, intensified, and slowly took shape. It was a face, vaguely familiar, speaking to me. The words were high pitched and slightly garbled, "Knee-eels, knee-eels, knee-eels."

The face moved in and out of view several times and then faded altogether. The squawking continued. I opened my eyes; seagulls were circling overhead. A Great Blue Heron landed in the shallow water in front of me. The long-legged bird looked like a prehistoric animal, a holdout from another time on planet earth. The smell of salt air tickled my memory.

I jumped to my feet. The startled heron took flight, its single cry of protest echoing across Eld Inlet. My mind followed the sound before returning to the beach. I wandered up and down the shoreline and called out José Humevo's name. There was no reply. I threw some water on my face to clear my head and hiked the trail back to campus.

My afternoon class was already in session. I was late, again. I must have slept longer than I realized. I attempted to follow the discussion circling around the room, but my thoughts were somewhere else. After class I checked the bench in Red Square. It was empty, not unlike the feeling in my belly. I went home, crawled into bed, and slept for sixteen hours.

For the next few days José Humevo was foremost on my mind. I thought about the portals, the *principles of learning*, and his acronym for *fear*. I could see his piercing eyes, hear his rhythmic voice, and feel his free-spirited laughter reverberating inside me. I checked the bench in Red Square again and again but José Humevo was nowhere to be found.

TRANSITIONS

◆

Marisa Taylor caught my attention immediately. She approached me wearing work boots, a short pleated skirt, and a jean jacket. Closer inspection revealed a white camisole peeking out beneath a partially unbuttoned flannel shirt. It was the first day at my new work/study job in the library and Marisa had been assigned to show me around.

The two of us shared a common work schedule and more often than not I found myself gravitating to where ever she happened to be working. I loved her smile, her laughter, her individuality. As the weeks passed I began to spend more of my free time with her as well. The attraction appeared to be mutual but I allowed the local mores to keep me from pursuing anything beyond causal flirting.

I had transferred to Evergreen mid year and one of the first things I noticed was an odd tension between the

male and the female students and some language guide-
lines that were socially reinforced. After a couple of repri-
mands I learned to never use the word *girl* to refer to any
female over the age of twelve.

During the course of the year, a small group of
women, who called themselves womyn, had managed to
create an atmosphere on campus where it was considered
politically incorrect to be in an openly heterosexual relationship. This took me by surprise, but I was new to the
environment and took my cues externally. I ignored my gut
instincts and got in line with the rest of the sheep.

My sexual frustration eventually brought me to my
senses. Marisa and I met at a party and after three hours of
non-stop talking decided that it was time to spend the
night together. The feel of her soft skin and the scent of her
body melted me in a way I had never experienced before. I
couldn't believe that I had allowed the prevailing social
order to dampen my expressions of affection for her. I
laughed at myself for being so easily influenced and made
a point of holding her hand in an exaggerated manner
every time we crossed Red Square. Marisa expressed her
dissent with humor. She showed me a card that she was
sending to a professor whose wife had just given birth to
their first child. Inside the card she had written,
"Congratulations on your new baby woman."

The school year came to an end and Marisa was
preparing to leave for a nine-month internship in Europe.
We were both ready for a break from campus life and decided to explore the San Juan Islands together. It was the perfect opportunity for a quick romantic get-away. We headed

out of Olympia on Interstate 5, stopping in Stanwood to visit my parents, Albert and Olga. Marisa's quirky sense of humor won them over immediately and they invited us to spend the night, separate bedrooms of course. House rules.

In the morning we took the ferry from Anacortes and cruised through the lush green water of the San Juans. It looked like liquid emeralds all around us. An hour and fifteen minutes later we departed the ferry at Orcas Landing and drove to Moran State Park where we hiked and swam, ate and talked, played and relaxed. Marisa's dark brown eyes created a tingling sensation in my chest that brought back fond memories of puppy love.

After two bliss-filled days on Orcas Island we caught the international ferry to Sidney, British Columbia where we looked up Lance and Gretchen, friends of mine from high school. They welcomed us into their home in Victoria and showed us the sights of south Vancouver Island. The four of us hiked to a secluded mountain lake and swam naked in the clear blue water. Lance and I reminisced about old times while Marisa and Gretchen walked around the lake. When I mentioned being on Orcas, Lance asked if I'd seen Rob Retlef, another friend from Stanwood.

"When did he move to Orcas?"

"About a year ago. He's building log cabins with some guy on the island."

'Really? I'd love to see him."

"I've got his address back at the house. Remind me to give it to you before you leave."

Rob was one of the most generous people I had ever known. Somewhere along the way we had lost track of one another. I didn't realize until that moment how much I had missed his steadfast friendship. Lance ran back to the water, his white butt glistening in the sun. I laughed out loud and followed him into the lake.

The next morning I got Rob's address, we exchanged hugs all around, and Marisa and I headed back to Sidney. It was a leisurely cruise to Anacortes. Marisa took a nap and I wrote a long letter to Rob. Clouds gathered in the Strait of Juan de Fuca and passed directly overhead on their way to the foothills of the Cascade Mountains. I walked outside and could smell the rain in the air ten minutes before it began to sprinkle. The ferry unloaded and we made the long drive back to Olympia as twilight settled over Puget Sound.

Two days later, I drove Marisa to the airport. With mutual sadness and understanding we agreed to officially end our brief romantic relationship. I waited in the corridor staring at the airplane as it taxied away from the terminal, lifted off the tarmac, and disappeared into the clouds.

The assumption that I would simply continue on my merry way turned out to be inaccurate. The sound of her laughter, the touch of her hand, and the scent of her body drifted in and out of my thoughts as the weeks and months rolled by. The camaraderie I had enjoyed with Marisa and the other students in the library was painfully absent. The program I had enrolled in was less than inspiring and I moved listlessly through the heat of summer, feeling like a radiator leaking water through a gaping hole.

The quarter finally ground to a halt and I called my parents to check in. They invited me to join them for a week in the San Juans. They were avid boaters who loved spending time on the water in their small cruiser, the *Alga*, a combination of their names – Albert and Olga. Their little dog, Fluffy, wore a blue and white sailor suit while boating. My mom thought it was adorable. I found it embarrassing.

We agreed to meet in Friday Harbor. It was a gorgeous day as I boarded the ferry in Anacortes. Sitting on deck, my mind turned to Marisa. The afternoon sun warmed my body, memories of the past warmed my heart, and the disappointments of the long, lonely summer began to melt away.

I found the *Alga* in the boat harbor next to the ferry terminal on San Juan Island. Fluffy was on the dock, her sailor suit slightly askew. I pointed this out to my mother who made the necessary adjustments. She welcomed me onboard, and immediately put me to work. We set the table and made a salad while my dad grilled steaks on his miniature hibachi. After dinner we played a rousing game of Yatzee and called it a night. I slept in the bow of the boat and enjoyed the gentle rocking as I drifted off to sleep.

In the morning, I crawled out of bed, walked to the stern of the boat, and dove into the chilly water of Friday Harbor. The hoot I let out upon reaching the surface brought more smiles than glares from the surrounding boaters, so I surmised that I was still within the bounds of proper mariner etiquette. My early morning dip became a ritual for me over the next few days.

We hopped from island to island. The weather was clear, the food abundant, the conversations easy, most of the time. When Albert and Olga asked me about school I quickly changed the subject. I was seriously thinking about taking a break and suspected that they would not approve. I had only recently surfaced from the lost years, an extended period of hitchhiking up and down the west coast, trips to Alaska, short stints at odd jobs, and long periods without communication home. I wandered, I meditated, I did yoga, all in an attempt to find myself, all apparently in vain. School, no school, it didn't seem to matter. My direction remained unclear.

We crossed the Canadian boarder and spent the night on Saturna Island. During my morning dip I noticed a man on a nearby dock waving a frozen fish back and forth over his head. As I attempted to figure out what he was doing, he tossed the fish high into the air. It flipped end over end and landed thirty feet from where I was treading water.

A bald eagle swooped down, extended his massive wings to slow his descent, and snatched the fish with his talons right in front of me. The sound and the pressure from his beating wings washed over me as he worked to gain altitude. He tilted his head and stared directly into my eye. The look was both magical and unnerving.

My dad had witnessed the entire episode and we excitedly shared the experience with my mother who was still in bed having coffee. After breakfast we pulled anchor and cruised back into U.S. water. Our destination was Deer Harbor on Orcas Island. Once we tied up, I found a phone booth and called Rob Retlef. He seemed surprised to hear my voice.

"Where are you?" he asked.

"I'm in Deer Harbor."

"Really? My cabin is only a couple of miles away, I can be there in five minutes."

"I'll wait at the end of the dock."

Rob pulled into the marina parking lot in his '52 GMC pickup, jumped out and gave me a warm embrace. He hadn't changed a bit, the ever-present baseball cap, the horn rim glasses resting on the end of his nose, the congenial smile. I took him down to the *Alga* to see my parents and the three of them chatted over coffee. When he heard they were cruising back to Stanwood, Rob invited me to stay with him for a few days. We had a late lunch on the boat before helping the *Alga* cast off. My mom waved as they trolled out of the harbor.

Rob and I climbed into his beautiful old truck, Lucy. He was in the process of restoring her and she was in that perfect place between being funky enough to actually use on a daily basis and classy enough to turn heads wherever she went. Rob was an ace mechanic. Lucy was his pride and joy.

We drove to the top of Mount Constitution and took in the amazing 360-degree view of the San Juan Archipelago and the snow-capped mountains beyond. We sat in the sun and traded stories. In contrast to my life, Rob had clear intentions and goals. He was saving money to buy land and had already started sketching house plans. I longed for a home in the country and was envious of his focus and resolve.

When I shared my dissatisfaction with school, Rob

started to grin.

"My boss has been looking for someone to peel logs."

"Really?"

"Yeah, you interested?"

"Uh-huh." My head nodded up and down.

"You could stay with me for awhile and see how you like it. We're starting a new project in about a week." His eyes twinkled. "Let's check it out."

Next thing I knew we were back in Lucy descending the curvy mountain road on our way to meet Ken Stevens, the owner of Authentic Log Cabins. The stoic expression on his chiseled face was difficult to read. He looked like Clint Eastwood, sizing me up without saying a word. I felt like a used car under inspection. Is he going to come over and feel my biceps? Finally, he spoke.

"The logs won't come until week after next. I can't guarantee long term work but you are welcome to start and see where it leads."

"Great."

Rob and Ken started talking about some work-related matter and I drifted off, day dreaming about the future. Rob nudged me on his way back to the truck. We said goodbye to Ken, bounced down the road in Lucy, and talked non-stop late into the evening.

The following morning I returned to Olympia and moved out of my student apartment, packed my work clothes and my camping gear, and gave everything else away. It was refreshing to let go of the past and move forward with a lighter load. The low-level tension that I had been carrying around for the past several months vanished as I drove out of town. I rolled down the windows, cranked up the stereo, and let the wind blow through my hair as I cruised towards the future.

PLAN G

♦

I ARRIVED ON Orcas ready to go but the work was not ready for me. I used the free time to explore the island and look for a place of my own. Rob was a good friend but his cabin was small and I didn't want to overstay my welcome. I had lived with friends before and understood that good friends and good housemates were not necessarily synonymous. The summer rentals were still occupied but looking for a place to live was a great way to explore the island. I kept my eyes and ears open and practiced patience. I knew the right place would show up.

The logs arrived and were piled in the corner of the abandoned gravel pit that Authentic Log Cabins called home. Rob introduced me to his co-worker, Nate, who had grown up on Orcas and was a true country boy. He was long and lean with a head of curly hair and a thick black beard. His friendly smile and easy disposition helped me feel right at home. The three of us stood around talking until Ken raced in, shouted a few commands, and zoomed away as quickly as he had arrived. Nate looked at me and laughed.

"Welcome to Authentic Log Cabins."

Rob escorted me to my work station and showed me what to do. My job was to remove the bark from the logs before they were moved into place with the boom truck and hand-notched to fit together. Rob and Nate would be notching. I would be peeling logs, lots of logs. The tool I was handed was called a log spud, which looked like a garden hoe that had been flattened out and sharpened on the leading edge.

After a quick tutorial I began my career as a log spudder. The trick was to get underneath the bark with the edge of the spud and push it forward with both hands, both arms, both legs and any other body part willing to join in. I learned rather rapidly that all logs are not created equal. Some logs peel relatively easily and some logs do not. This particular batch had precious few of the former. By noon my arms felt like they were going to fall off my body. I was not altogether certain that I would be able to lift my sandwich to my mouth when we stopped for lunch. Rob noticed my weariness and told me to take the afternoon off.

"It takes a few days to get used to spudding."

"But what if Ken comes back and I'm not here?"

"Trust me, he'll understand. We've all been there before."

I wanted to make a good impression with Ken, but

I wasn't about to argue with Rob on this one. I was happy to call it a day.

The next morning I woke up and attempted to get out of bed. The first thing I noticed was that movement of any kind was not a pleasurable experience. I took a hot shower to loosen up before heading off to work. The stiffness in my body subsided as my muscles warmed up and began to relax. I worked for six hours the second day and eight hours the day after that. I was still sore but the soreness had shifted from something I tried to avoid to something I wanted more of.

By the end of the week I could see, as well as feel, my body getting stronger. I was pleased with myself. It would have been easy to quit after that first morning but I hung in there and pushed through the initiation period. Rob and I celebrated on Friday night with dinner at the Chinese Restaurant in Eastsound.

The next two weeks looked much like the first, me on spud detail, Rob and Nate notching logs, Ken buzzing in and out all the time. It was easy for me to hang out with Rob and Nate. Ken, on the other hand, was an enigma. He was only five years older than me, but seemed like he belonged to a different generation. At first I thought he had it all together. He had a loving family, a beautiful home, his own business, an airplane, a boat, and a fleet of wheeled vehicles. He was living his dream.

However, the more I watched him the more scattered he appeared to be. He would change plans all day long. Nate, in a rather deadpan manner, referred to this as plan G, meaning that we had already worked our way through plans A, B, C, D, E, and F on any given day. This amused me at first, but the novelty wore off rather quickly. The same was true for peeling logs. What had been new and exciting the first week of work began to lose its charm.

After three weeks on the job, my muscles were strong and firm but my spirit was beginning to waver. As I repeatedly pushed the bark off an endless supply of logs, college life began to look more and more attractive. Fortunately, or unfortunately, I'm not sure which, fall quarter had already started. Going back to school was no longer an option. I had made a decision to come to Orcas to work and save money, and that is what I needed to do. That's what I kept telling myself anyway.

On Monday morning of week four I was back at the gravel pit spudding away when Nate pulled in and yelled from the cab of his truck.

"Drop yer spud, boy, you've been promoted!"

"What do you mean by promoted?"

"You're coming with us to Henry Island. Let's go."

"All right!" I grabbed my lunch and jumped into Nate's truck. He put it in gear and we raced to the Eastsound airfield.

Henry is a small island just across the channel from Roche Harbor on the West Side of San Juan Island. Ken had built a cabin on Henry Island that was in the final stages of completion and there was a push to get it done. Rob and Nate had been going to Henry Island, on and off for the last couple of weeks, leaving me alone at the pit much of the time. I was more than happy to join them.

We met Ken and Rob at the airfield and climbed

into Ken's vintage four-passenger airplane. The cramped quarters of the cockpit rattled as we sped down the runway. The noise was irritating and the smell of fuel permeated the cabin, but it was better than peeling logs. The sight of the blue-green water and rocky shorelines below enthralled me as the plane climbed higher and higher.

Our plan was to land on the beach on Henry Island. However, this being an Authentic Log Cabin outing, plans were subject to change. Halfway to Henry Island the wind picked up and Ken decided that it would be safer to land at Friday Harbor. He kept an old car at the airport and we all piled in. Ken drove us across San Juan Island to Roche Harbor where our next mode of transportation awaited. It was a wooden vessel that looked like a miniature tugboat. It appeared to be older than the airplane. Once again, we moved our gear and ourselves from one antique vehicle to another.

The crossing from Roche Harbor to Henry Island was not far, perhaps a thousand yards. We made half that distance before the diesel engine sputtered to a halt and refused to start. While Rob attempted to fix the engine, Ken pulled out a small outboard motor and used it to get us the rest of the way across the channel. He pulled too close to shore while dropping us off and sheared the pin on the outboard propeller.

Rob, Nate, and I walked to the cabin while Ken pulled out some oars and began to row the boat back to Roche Harbor for repairs. Ken had a love affair with old machinery that he managed to keep on the positive side of just barely functioning. It was a delicate dance, but with duct tape and dumb luck he pulled it off again and again. I was waiting to see what he was going to do if the oars broke on the way back to civilization. The guy was resourceful if nothing else.

Nate and I climbed onto the roof and started laying hand-split cedar shakes while Rob took the boom truck into the woods to get more logs. Boomer, as we affectionately called him, was a World War II army truck with a fifteen-foot boom and winch attached to the front end. The boys had barged Boomer to Henry Island a week earlier in order to pull shake bolts out of the forest. Out of all of Ken's toys, Boomer was my favorite.

Everything was going great until Boomer got stuck in the woods. Nate and I responded to Rob's call for help and found Boomer axle deep in mud. It took the three of us forty-five minutes to extract him from the quagmire. The wind continued to blow. Nate and I got back on the roof and did our best to keep our tools and our bodies from flying away in the gusting wind. An hour later we heard the toot-toot-toot of a boat horn and saw Ken approaching the island. We yelled to Rob and headed for the beach.

The journey back to Roche Harbor was an event in itself. The whitecaps on the water slammed against our tiny vessel and bounced it around like a cork in a stream. It was slow going across the channel and slower still to successfully dock the boat. As we drove to Friday Harbor the wind grew even stronger. The trees along the roadside were flexing wildly back and forth. A large fir tree snapped in the wind and crashed on the road in front of us. The thud vibrated up through the tires. We waited until a local logger with bright orange suspenders cut a swath for us to drive through. The delay made us late for the ferry. The next boat was three hours away. All of us were tired, hungry, and anxious to get home. Ken decided to fly back to Orcas in spite of the weather.

I had been in a small plane only once before that morning so I wasn't exactly sure what the limitations of an antique four-passenger airplane might be. When a violent gust of wind blew out the Plexiglas window next to my head I concluded that we were rapidly approaching those limitations. The loud pop and sudden blast of wind against my face sent a shiver of fear through my entire body. I could feel the pounding of my heart against my hands as they instinctively gripped the safety harness strapped tightly across my chest. My tense posture and exaggerated breathing were not particularly helpful to Ken who was wrestling with the controls in the seat next to mine.

My stomach churned as another blast of wind rocked the plane and we suddenly lost altitude. I caught the scent of burning oil as the over-burdened engine struggled to keep up. The rapidly approaching water that I had found so enthralling earlier in the day now took on a more menacing look. The metallic taste of fear filled my mouth. My body broke out in a cold sweat as several less than desirable scenarios filled my imagination. I felt myself tumbling down the rabbit hole of fear when the words of José Humevo grabbed me by the back of the neck.

"Either I run my fears or my fears run me."

Fear – Fantasized Experience Appearing Real. The scenarios I had created in my mind were becoming reality for my body. I was experiencing them as if they were real. I looked at Ken who was struggling to gain control of the airplane and realized that I was fighting just as hard to pull out of my own internal nose-dive. Something inside of me shifted and I accepted that there was nothing I could do about the fate of the airplane. I took a deep breath and eased my grip on the safety harness. I watched from a place of relative detachment as Ken made a series of rapid adjustments that stabilized the airplane. His ability to quickly change plans suddenly took on a whole new meaning as he skillfully guided us through the turbulence back to Orcas Island.

We let out a collective sigh of relief when the tires touched solid ground and rolled to a stop. There was nervous chatter between us as we tied down the wings and covered the plane for the night. Life at Authentic Log Cabins was always an adventure but this was one to remember. As it turned out we had flown home in the leading edge of a storm that would rock the islands for the next three days. The wind and the rain pounded San Juan County. I stayed close to the wood stove, drinking tea and catching up on my reading and writing. I also spent a fair amount of time thinking about José Humevo and wondering if I would ever see him again.

Rob spent most of his time at Ken's shop, tuning up chainsaws and trucks, sharpening axes and spuds. He truly was mister handyman. Rob liked to stay busy, but it was clear to me that he was also feeling a bit cramped in his own cabin. The sunshine returned and I went looking to find a place of my own. It took me less than an hour.

TRANSFORMATION

◆

TURTLEBACK LODGE WAS in a serious state of disrepair. It had the familiar musty smell of an old abandoned building. The floorboards squeaked as I moved around the dimly lit rooms. I stepped carefully onto the covered porch listing towards the shoreline twenty feet below and took in the view of the snow-capped mountains in the distance.

A bevy of small cabins surrounded the disheveled lodge. Their condition ranged from burn-it-down to move-right-in. This entire collection of buildings sat at the foot of Turtleback Mountain on the northwest coastline of Orcas Island. As I wandered around the property, I heard the laughter of small children and followed the sound to its source. I found three young blonde-headed girls playing on the beach, chasing one another and giggling wildly. Their parents were sitting in lounge chairs, sipping wine, and enjoying the expressions of freedom and joy that were swirling at their feet. I walked over and introduced myself.

Kerry and Kendra were from Victoria. They had recently purchased two of the Turtleback cabins as vacation property and this was their first weekend stay. After five minutes of conversation I discovered that they had bought the property from Nate's father, who was a realtor on the island, and that Lanny and Gretchen were clients at Kerry's dental practice in Victoria. Another chair and another wineglass appeared and we spent the next thirty minutes talking, laughing, and getting to know one another. By the time I departed I had become the caretaker of Kerry and Kendra's island property. They told me I could live in the smaller of the two cabins in exchange for minor repairs and keeping an eye on their investment.

Earlier that day I had felt the pressure building at Rob's cabin. Now I felt open, expansive, and free. Not unlike the children playing on the beach. After shaking hands with Kerry and Kendra to seal our agreement, I drove to Rob's cabin, left him a note and raced for the ferry.

I returned the following morning with a load of furniture and kitchen supplies from Albert and Olga's basement and spent the day unpacking boxes and arranging furniture in my new home. The rustic cabin had indoor plumbing, a river rock fireplace, and a cozy little bedroom. The interior walls were lined with wide plank cedar paneling. A row of small-paned windows opened to the spectacular view beyond. As darkness fell I noticed a new moon above the silhouette of distant mountains. I made a bowl of popcorn and sat in front of the fireplace with only the soft glow of the fire lighting the big smile on my face. I slept soundly that first night.

In the morning I opened the arched doorway that led to the outside deck and studied Patos Island, named by Spanish explorers in the late 1700's. I was doing some exploring of my own and decided to name my cabin, Casa de Nils. By the end of the week I had carved the name on a piece of driftwood and hung it on the front door.

I returned to work on Monday morning feeling like a new man. The storm had cleared, I had a new home, and I wasn't pushing a spud for eight hours a day any longer. Over the next couple of weeks we went back and forth between Orcas and Henry, sometimes by land, sometimes by sea, sometimes by air. I loved the first time we landed on the beach in front of the cabin on Henry Island. It was quite a thrill. I looked forward to flying over the San Juan Islands and was disappointed on the days when we took the ferry instead.

The job on Henry Island came to an end so it was back to the gravel pit to work on the next house. The routine was to build the shell of a house at the gravel pit where it was easy to drive Boomer all the way around the structure as it was being erected. Once the walls were up, we would mark the ends of the logs with metal tags indicating their order of placement, disassemble the whole thing, load it on a log truck and deliver it to the building site.

At that point it was simply a matter of finding the correct logs and stacking them back together again. It was one large jigsaw puzzle. Once the walls were up, we would cut out openings for the doors and windows with a chainsaw, frame up the roof structure, and do whatever finish work was required to complete the job. This pattern created a schedule where we would be at the gravel pit part of the time and at a job site part of the time. It was a pleasant rhythm that suited my desire for predictability as well as change.

Business picked up and Ken hired two young hippie-looking women and put them on spud duty. Their colorful clothing and shapely bodies were a pleasant addition to the starkness of the gravel pit. The new crew members did not wear bras. The sensual movement of breasts captivated Rob and Nate. They gawked like adolescent boys as Patti and Annie peeled their first log. I kept my head down and my eyes to myself. There was a piece of information that my male companions had yet to comprehend. Patti and Annie were lesbians.

They neither hid nor proclaimed their relationship. They expressed their love for one another with clarity and ease. They were not at all like the Evergreen womyn, who had obviously pushed a few of my buttons. It wasn't until I had put some distance between school and myself that I was able to see how passive I had been in Olympia. I was afraid I would be ostracized if I didn't toe the line at Evergreen. It was another glaring example of a Fantasized Experience Appearing Real. I told myself that I would not fall into that trap again.

Patti and Annie were delightful. They tempered our construction worker mentality and filled our days with laughter and song. Annie loved to sing; Patti was a trickster. We never knew what song or practical joke would be coming next.

Annie and I hit it off immediately. We had an easy rapport and spent hours talking about music, art, philosophy. We developed an intimacy without sexual tension. Patti was not at all threatened by the connection that Annie and I shared. She seemed to understand that our individual relationships with Annie were complimentary, not competitive. Patti's awareness caused me to cringe at the level of immaturity I had displayed in similar situations in the past.

Summer drifted into autumn, the nights grew longer, and work began to slow down. On rainy mornings the crew would gather at the Crow's Nest Café and decide what to do. Some days we would all go to the gravel pit, other days we would split up and head off in different directions, some days we would just drink coffee and go home. It all depended on the weather, the task at hand, the cycle of the moon. It changed from day to day.

I loved my days off. I puttered around my cabin, wrote letters to friends, read books, wrote in my journal. Annie and I took long walks on the beach. I enjoyed her youthful energy, her thoughtful questions, and her beautiful songs.

The winter solstice arrived and work continued to slow down. Patti and Annie decided to move on after Christmas, looking for warmer weather and more consistent work. Annie's departure left a hole in my heart. I spent New Year's Eve alone in my cabin and went to bed at 10:30 just to be contrary. Shotgun blasts and bottle rockets challenged my decision for the next few hours. The night fell silent around 2:00 am. I woke up late the next morning, walked outside and greeted 1979. I spent most of the day sitting on the beach, listening to the waves, and attempting to understand the restless feeling growing inside of me. One night several weeks later, I had a vivid dream.

I was in the ocean and there was a storm beginning to build. The water was churning and I was a long way from shore, struggling to keep my head above water, my strength rapidly waning. Just as I was about to give up, a giant eagle swooped down and grabbed me with its massive talons. It was frightening and a little painful to be in its clutches but I did not sense any ill intentions. The truth is that the eagle had just saved my life. My body was exhausted and gave itself over to the experience. My mind, however, continued to question if this was an out-of-the-frying-pan into-the-fire situation and I began to struggle. As I fought, the talons tightened around me. I relaxed and the grip softened once again. I told myself to relax. There is no malice here.

As we were flying, the eagle turned his head and looked directly into my eyes. It was a look I had seen before. I remembered the eagle in the harbor on Saturna Island and then I remembered standing by the bench in Red Square. As I was looking at the eagle, he became José Humevo. We were standing on a rocky beach surrounded by huge pieces of driftwood. Enormous waves were crashing on the shoreline. The roar was deafening. José Humevo was saying something but I couldn't understand him. I moved closer and he whispered in my ear, "It's time to wake up; time to discover the path within." He placed the palm of his hand on the center of my chest. "The place to look is here."

As he touched me, my heart began to glow, spreading warmth throughout my entire body. My physical self melted. I became heat and light radiating out into the vastness of the universe, expanding in so many directions that I could no longer hold my awareness of self. I let go of who I knew myself to be and as I released my grip, everything became nothing.

Slowly, I began to be aware of my body. I was lying in my bed, in my room, in my cabin. I was pulsating with energy and could feel the activity of my molecular structure. I watched myself shifting from a dreaming to a waking state, as if my consciousness was a fluid being poured from one level of awareness into another.

I did not move for a long time, not wanting to disrupt whatever was going on. Eventually the heat, the light, the glow inside my body began to dissipate and I returned to something that resembled normal waking reality. I felt expansive as I dressed, had breakfast, and drove to work. Rob was alone at the gravel pit when I pulled in. I jumped out of my car and started to tell him about my dream. He seemed half-asleep and mumbled that I had been reading too much Carlos Castaneda.

Rob's response took me by surprise. My expansive spirit shrunk to the size of a pea. I stepped back and raised my shields, wrapping myself in an all too familiar cloak of defensiveness and judgement. This knee-jerk reaction was comforting in an odd sort of way. As I retreated into old habits the memory of my dream came flooding back to me. My desire to learn and grow collided with the inertia of my constrictive self. I was back in the turbulent surf. This time it was a memory stored in that quiet place deep within my spirit, not the talons of an eagle, that lifted me from the turmoil.

"Taking anything too seriously is the one thing that will always trip us up." The words of José Humevo challenged my old unconscious behavior. Where was my humor and humility? Where were the stepping stones that would carry me forward? I looked at Rob. He was staring at me with a questioning look on his face.

"Are you okay?"

It took me a second to answer. "Uh-huh."

"Are you sure?"

"I'm fine," I said. "I was just trying to remember something."

"Hey, I was being sarcastic, you caught me off guard. I'd love to hear more about your dream."

I hesitated, and in that moment I could see the choice in front of me. Old pattern or new pattern, which would it be? I took a long breath, lowered my shields and started to share. It was clumsy at first, but the more I talked, the more I relaxed.

By the time Nate showed up, Rob and I were chopping away on a log, lost in conversation. The three of us settled into our routine of bantering as we worked. There were long periods of silence as well. I used the quiet time to reflect on the mysterious dream and the wide range of emotions I had experienced since crawling out of bed. It brought to mind one of the first concepts that José Humevo had shared. I was beginning to understand how opening or closing my portals directly affected the way I experienced anything – and everything.

LETTING GO

—————◆—————

WINTER GAVE WAY to spring, work picked up, and Ken hired a new crew member, Ed Dicks. By the end of the first week I started calling him Ed's Dick because his motivating goal in life was to have sex with a hundred women before his thirtieth birthday. He proudly proclaimed this to me on more than one occasion. Ed was approaching twenty-nine and still had a ways to go. He was getting a little nervous, a little more desperate, and a lot more obnoxious in his approach. Having sex with women was a sport for him. It was all about getting another notch in his belt. Wham-bam-thank-you-ma'am.

Ed was a Viet Nam vet. He wore camouflage pants to work every day. The sleeves of his army surplus tee shirts had all been cropped to give his massive arms room to move. He kept his hair in a ponytail and a Camel cigarette in his mouth at all times. Ed loved to talk about sports – football, baseball, and basketball – in that order. He called skiing, gymnastics, and tennis sissy sports. Women or sports, that's about as far as it went. He was boring to converse with but fascinating to observe. Ed was the fastest notcher I had ever seen. He could make a chainsaw sing and an axe dance. His addition to the crew rearranged the pecking order and I found myself pushing a spud more often than not.

One rainy morning in mid June, Ed and I were alone at the gravel pit working on the walls of a new house. He was going on about his latest conquest and I was lost in some reverie of my own, ignoring his endless babble. I started to climb down the eight-foot high wall. My foot slipped on a wet log, I lost my balance and tumbled backwards, my arms flailing as I attempted to land on my feet. I was not successful. The hollow thud from my body hitting the ground caught Ed's attention. He turned to see what had happened.

"You all right?"

"I think so."

As I stood up I noticed blood dripping on the ground. I checked my body and saw a hunk of flesh dangling from the lower part of my left thumb.

"Shit!"

I had sliced myself with my freshly sharpened Hudson Bay axe on the way down. Ed saw the blood and jumped off the wall in one fluid movement. He looked like Batman flying towards me in slow motion. The next thing I knew, Ed had my hand wrapped in his tee shirt, my arm above my head, and we were on our way to town. He joked with me on the way, but I could see the look of concern on his face.

The cut required ten stitches but there was no damage to tendon or bone. I left the doctor's office with a prescription for Percodan and instructions to rest, relax, and recuperate. Ed took me home and helped me get settled. He and Rob brought my car over later that day. They brought some food, made sure I had everything I needed and then left me alone. I thanked Ed for his help and concern. I had experienced a side of him that I had not taken the time to notice before. I never called him Ed's Dick again.

I cried that night for the first time in a long while. Not so much from the physical pain as from the emotional wound that the accident had opened up. It felt like I had just been handed a snapshot of my life and the picture was not entirely satisfying. The Percodan kicked in and I fell into a deep sleep. I awoke in the morning with two puffy eyes, one throbbing hand, and a head full of unanswered questions.

A long hot shower washed the sleep from my eyes and temporarily cleared my mind. I stood naked on the deck and noticed a strange movement in the distant water. It took me a moment to realize that it was a pod of Orca whales coming my way. I grabbed my binoculars and for the next ten minutes watched an amazing show.

There were 12 - 15 Orcas of various sizes rolling, jumping, and splashing as they made their way toward me. The males had tall black dorsal fins that towered above the others. All of the large black and white mammals were rolling and splashing and spouting as they cruised in front of my cabin, but the males were something else. Occasionally, they would jump completely out of the water, rotate 90 degrees, and come crashing down on their massive sides. This movement made a huge splash in the water. I would see the splash and then hear the sound a second later. The display of beauty, grace, and power held my attention until the whales disappeared behind Point Doughty. Things might not be perfect, but I was still living in paradise.

The excitement of the whale sighting slowly faded and was replaced by the questions that had greeted me upon waking. I felt split down the middle. Half of me wanted to hunker down in paradise and keep saving money. Half of me felt like it was time to go back to school. It seemed like the grass was always greener wherever I was not. I felt like I had one shoe nailed to the floor; no matter how much energy I put out, I still kept going around and around in circles.

After a week of navel gazing I had my stitches removed but the very center of the cut was not completely healed. The doctor sealed it with a butterfly bandage and told me to give it a few more days. The island felt claustrophobic so I jumped in my car and headed for Olympia. The long drive gave me an opportunity to think about my dream, my accident, my future. There was something stirring inside of me, just beyond my reach.

When I got to Evergreen I went straight to Red Square. I told myself I was going to the library but I made a point to walk by the bench, just in case. I pretended not to see the empty bench, pretended not to feel the disappointment inside of me.

I spent three days in Olympia, hanging out on campus and talking with friends. I only had one year of school left and it all started to look more attractive to me. A new program that was being offered in the fall caught my attention. I took a copy of the program description and an application to re-apply for admission. I picked up the latest copy of the *Cooper Point Journal*, the school newspaper, and headed out of town. My mind was full of questions as I drove to Anacortes.

The following week I was back at work, pushing a spud. My hand was feeling tender and my spirit wasn't much into peeling logs. My work days were short and uninspiring. On Wednesday morning I pulled into the pit and started working. I couldn't figure out why everyone was acting a little weird. Ken arrived and sent Rob, Nate, and Ed to the job site. After they left he informed me that the next house had fallen through and that there wasn't enough work to keep everybody busy.

"Somebody has to go and I've decided it's you."

"What?" It took a second for his words to register. "Why not Ed? I've been here longer than he has."

Ken's jaw stiffened. "That's just the way it is. I'm sorry if you're bent out of shape."

There was an awkward silence between us.

"Today doesn't have to be your last day, you can work until the end of the pay period if you want." He got in his truck and left. The end of the pay period was three days away.

"Thanks for the generous notice."

I flipped Ken off as he drove away and threw my spud across the gravel pit. I yelled out every swear word that I knew with amazing rapidity and force and didn't stop until my voice gave out. I put my tools away and went looking for someone to talk to. It didn't help that I couldn't find anyone to fill that bill. The sad truth was that my main community on Orcas Island revolved around work. With that lifeline being severed, I felt completely lost.

Rob stopped by after work and we had a good talk. He told me that Ken hadn't enjoyed our encounter anymore than I had. He was feeling the money crunch from losing the next project. I was the first person he had ever laid off and Ken admitted to Rob that he had done an awkward job of it. I thanked Rob for the additional perspective and went to bed feeling better than I had earlier in the day.

The next morning I showed up at work early and was spudding away as the rest of the crew pulled in. I think they were surprised to see me and even more surprised by my attitude. I had had my little tizzy fit (in private, thankfully) and was now ready to accept my fate. Once I got beyond my bruised ego, I realized that Ed was indeed more valuable to Ken than I was. I had decided to make the most of my last few days on the job.

I don't know if it was my shift in attitude or what, but Ken found work for me to do. He made an attempt to keep me busy. I worked on and off over the next few weeks but eventually it became clear to both of us that he was trying a little too hard. We had another talk and by the end of our conversation it was obvious that it was time for me to end my employment with Authentic Log Cabins. We parted on much better terms.

Rob told me about a guy who was looking for help doing boat repair. I drove to the marina and found the man I was looking for. His name was Swede. He was a stocky man with kind eyes who reminded me of my father. He hired me on the spot. Most of our time was spent working on other people's boats, stripping, repairing, and painting hulls. Part of the time I helped Swede with his own boat, a forty-five foot wooden sailboat that he had been working on for over ten years.

Swede's wife had gotten a job in Seattle and had moved off the island about a month before I started working with him. She was happy in Seattle. He wanted to stay on Orcas. They would see each other on the weekends but it was not an ideal situation for either of them.

After a few weeks on the job, I showed up on a Monday morning ready to continue where we had left off before our weekend break. I found Swede standing in front of the barn where he was building his boat. There was a chainsaw at his feet and a huge pile of ashes in front of him.

"What are you burning, Swede?"

He was staring down at the smoldering ashes. "My boat."

"Come on, what did you really burn?"

He raised his head to look at me. "My boat. I got back from Seattle last night, took out my chainsaw and cut it up. I burnt it one piece at a time, it took me all night."

I thought he was joking. I walked over to the barn,

opened the door and let out a gasp – the barn was empty. He really had burnt his sailboat!

"But why?"

"That damn boat has been a chain around my neck for ten years. It was a dream that had turned into a nightmare. It was keeping me trapped on this island and it was ruining my marriage. On my way back from Seattle I decided that it was time to cut myself free from its spell."

"Why didn't you sell it or give it away?"

"I had to destroy it before it destroyed me. It was the only way. You are still young, Nils. Perhaps one day you will understand."

I was speechless. Swede was right; it would be a while before I fully appreciated his actions, but I did catch a glimpse of his logic that morning.

"I'm going to finish the job we're working on and then I'm closing the shop and moving to Seattle. My relationship with my wife is more important to me than my relationship with my customers and it is certainly more important than that *fucking boat*!"

Swede smiled after accentuating his final words, I could see the burden being lifted from his shoulders. We both laughed. By the end of the week, Swede and I finished our last job and delivered the boat to its owner. We packed up his shop and drove to Seattle. He put his tools in storage, moved into his wife's apartment, and started looking for work. We parted with a firm handshake, each wishing the other well.

I headed back to Anacortes. The drive provided an opportunity to ponder my next move. I had just lost my second job in less than a month but for some reason I was not the least bit concerned. While I sat in the parking lot waiting for the ferry to arrive, I dug around my car for something to read and found the *Cooper Point Journal* that I had picked up at Evergreen. The newspaper had fallen under my seat and I had forgotten all about it. I started reading, catching up on some old school news. I turned to the literary page and found the following poem:

The OmniBus

Where this bus is heading
I don't really know
The reason for the journey
May simply be to go

The road can be a challenge
The path not always clear
The way to keep on moving
Is to face your fear

The world's not out to get us
It wants to *get us out*
Free from limitation
Disbelief and doubt

Trusting is the secret
Courage is the way
Magic, awe, and mystery
Surround us every day

Open up the window
Set your spirit free
Embrace the world around you
It's another way to be

— J.H. Bozo

J.H. Bozo? I read the poem again, a little more carefully this time, put down the paper and laughed. José Humevo was still out there and it was time for me to find him. A vivid dream, a scarred hand, two lost jobs, and a big pile of ashes; what else would it take for me to get the message that perhaps it was time to let go of what I thought I wanted in order to find something of even greater value?

AN INVITATION

◆

As soon as I decided that it was time to leave Orcas the pieces all fell into place. Rob took over my caretaking responsibilities at Turtleback. I packed up, gave the place a thorough cleaning, and spent my final night in the cabin with the lights off. I sat in front of the fireplace, eating a bowl of popcorn and reminiscing about my time on Orcas Island. It was exactly like my first night in the cabin except that I felt older, wiser and ready to move on.

In the morning I walked outside and closed the door to Casa de Nils for the last time. I wandered around the property, taking it all in, before spending a few minutes on the beach, stretched out on my favorite rock. I met Ken Stevens at the Crow's Nest for breakfast. Our relationship had never been easy, but I was leaving feeling more like a man and wanted to thank him for his part in my growth. He seemed touched by the acknowledgement and gave me a hug as we said good-bye. It was our one and only embrace.

On my way to the ferry I saw things I had not noticed before – the shape of a tree, the color of the mailboxes, a subtle curve in the road. Everything seemed brighter, clearer, more enhanced. I arrived at the ferry terminal early and was the first car in line. Once I boarded the boat, I walked to the upper deck to watch the other cars loading. Just before the gate went down, a young woman came running towards the ferry. She ran like a gazelle. I had never seen anyone move with such grace and ease before. I followed her movement until she disappeared on the car deck below me.

As the ferry pulled away from Orcas, I moved inside and crossed paths with the gazelle woman. We exchanged smiles in passing and I felt myself blush. There was something about her that stirred me. It wasn't her beauty, although I did find her attractive. It was something I could not name. She stood on the rear deck of the boat, her long pigtails blowing in the wind. She was nineteen or twenty years old, tall and slender and full of life. I could not take my eyes off her. I felt compelled to talk with her but held myself back. I was leaving the San Juans, it was no time to be pursuing a woman.

The ferry made the short crossing from Orcas to Shaw Island and as the boat pulled into the slip, the gazelle woman ran by me and headed back to the car deck. I moved to the front of the boat and watched as she walked off the ferry and was greeted by the nuns who run the ferry terminal on Shaw. On the back of her tee shirt was printed *Shaw*

Island Spanish Camp – Staff.

    The gazelle woman was talking with the nuns as the three cars waiting in line drove on board. I felt a strange sense of loss as the gate closed and the ferry pulled away from the dock. As the distance between us increased my feeling of loss magnified and I surprised myself by yelling in her direction, "What's your name?" All three women looked up and I yelled again, "What's your name?"

    The gazelle woman pointed to herself with a questioning look on her face. I nodded my head enthusiastically and repeated, "What's your name?" She hesitated for a moment and then yelled back. The ferry engine was churning to bring the boat up to speed and I couldn't hear her reply. I held my hand to my ear and she yelled again but by this time we were too far apart. All I could do was wave good-bye. She returned the gesture. We were still waving to one another as the ferry changed course and an outcropping of land blocked her from my sight.

    My arm dropped to my side and my spirit dropped as well. I didn't know what to make of the empty feeling in my chest. It was such an odd encounter, so fleeting and yet so impactful. I told myself that I was simply feeling the emotion of leaving Orcas but that explanation did not totally satisfy me. I stood out on deck for a long time taking in the magic and wonder of the natural beauty around me, and all the while, the image of the gazelle woman kept seeping into my awareness. A small voice inside my head questioned my decision to leave but I knew it was time to go. I held firm to my decision.

    In less than week I had moved into a house on the

West Side of Olympia with my old ski buddy, Tammy Howard. We had met two years earlier when I answered her ad in the newspaper looking for a carpool to the mountains. Tammy was six feet tall, muscular, and could kick my butt on the slopes. We shared an irreverent sense of humor and love for downhill skiing. She had leased a one-bedroom house for the school year and was looking for a way to lower her rent.

After checking the place out I decided to move into the pantry. It was a 6x8-foot room directly off the kitchen and I converted it into a cozy little nest for myself. I built a bed platform on top of a set of dresser drawers that I found at the Goodwill and filled the pantry shelves with my books, my outdoor gear, and my sacred objects. I loved my tiny quarters; it was like living on a boat. Everything was neat, orderly, and within reach. The practical side of my Scandinavian nature was content.

Fall quarter began and I embraced my senior year of college with a gusto that I had not previously displayed. I kept one eye on my studies and one eye on the bench in Red Square each and every day. I checked the student enrollment list, the faculty roster, the phone book. Nothing panned out. I had moments of disappointment but they did not last long. Overall, my disposition remained positive and I held onto my intention to find José Humevo.

The Evergreen womyn were back to their old tricks, but I no longer responded to their histrionics. Tammy was more hooked by them than I was. She called them the nazi chicks and loved to jerk their chain. She put a bumper sticker on the rear window of her car that stated in big bold letters, A HARD MAN IS GOOD TO FIND. The message may or may not have registered with her intended audience, but according to the stories she told me, it drove the truckers wild.

A few weeks into the quarter the womyn removed the contents of an entire art show that had been hung in the library by a male photography student. Some of the black and white photographs contained images of nude female bodies in nature. Clearly, they were art photos, not pornography. However, the womyn had been offended. They sent a communiqué to the *Cooper Point Journal* stating that they had confiscated and destroyed the offensive sexist material.

The response from students and faculty alike was overwhelmingly negative. The womyn had finally crossed the line. Their tactics had backfired and the mysterious influence they had held on campus melted like a snowball in summer. The politically correct behavior that had been seeping into Evergreen's social fabric had finally reached the tipping point and collapsed into a pile of rubble.

I had been playing racquetball in the gym since the beginning of the quarter and was improving my agility and coordination. I loved to relax in the sauna after working up a sweat on the court. One day shortly after the confiscation incident, I walked into the sauna and found Jackson Barnes sitting on one of the benches, wrapped in a towel.

Jackson, a British mountaineer, was on his way to becoming the first person to successfully climb all fourteen 8K peaks, the world's highest mountains above 8000 meters. He was attempting his eleventh ascent when he was caught in a white out near the top of Annapurna in Nepal. It took all his strength, experience, and willpower to make it back to base camp. The fierce winds and freezing temperatures pounded his tent for three days.

Jackson endured the seventy-two hour ordeal but it was a costly experience. Nine of his severely frostbitten toes had to be amputated two weeks later in Katmandu. His ten-year career as a Himalayan mountain guide came to an abrupt end. He packed up his love for pushing himself and others to the edge and carried it back to academia. His path eventually led to the Evergreen State College where he was teaching a course entitled *Experiential Learning*.

Jackson had sky-blue eyes, a close cropped beard, and a full head of hair that was always slightly unkempt. His inquisitive mind constantly ran at full throttle. Years of hanging out with Buddhist monks had tempered, but not extinguished, his passion for adventure and learning.

We had never been formally introduced but I knew who he was. On more than one occasion I had seen him walking around the locker room barefoot, no toes on one foot and one lone big toe on the other. Most people would find it difficult to walk without toes. Jackson still played racquetball with the best of them and continued to spend time in the mountains.

We struck up a conversation about the recent campus uproar and had a good laugh about the absurdity of it all. After a short silence, he said, "It never works when a small group of people attempt to force their values on a larger social order. Oppression is still oppression whether it comes from the left, the right, or the center. Given enough time it always implodes from its own weight."

I appreciated his perspective. He articulated what I was feeling but had been unable to put into words. We sat in silence for awhile before he got up to leave.

"I enjoyed talking with you." He extended his right hand. "I'm Jackson."

"I know who you are." I matched his firm handshake. "My name is Nils."

"Nice to meet you, Nils." Jackson smiled, let go of my hand and headed for the door. He stopped and looked back at me as I was stretching out on the sauna bench.

"Are you Nils Christiansen?"

"Yes, how do you know my name?"

"Oh, we have a mutual friend."

"Who's that?" I knew a couple of students in Jackson's *Experiential Learning* Program, but none who would have had any reason to talk with him about me.

Jackson's smile grew even larger. "José Humevo."

"What?"

"José Humevo, we have been friends for years. He mentioned that he had met you when he was visiting a year or so ago. He had to leave on short notice and left a letter for you. He asked me to pass it on if we ever happened to cross paths. I'm sure I still have it in my office."

I was speechless. Jackson chuckled, not unlike José Humevo.

"I've got to go, but if you would like to come by my office tomorrow morning I'll see if I can find that letter. We can talk more at that time. Does 10:00 work for you?"

"Sure."

Jackson chuckled again, told me his office number, and closed the sauna door. I heard him yell from the other side, "See you tomorrow!"

The following morning I was outside Jackson's office at 10:00 am sharp. I could hear the muffled tones of a conversation on the other side of the door. After a few minutes a student walked out and Jackson made a hand motion to invite me in. He was writing something and took a moment before he looked up to greet me.

"Good morning, Nils, how are you today?"

"Great, and yourself?"

"Fine, fine." Jackson shuffled through a stack of papers on his desk. He held up an envelope and handed it to me. "From José Humevo."

I took the letter and stared at it. Part of me wanted to tear it open right then and there but another part of me wanted to wait, to be able to savor it in private. I was dying to know his connection with José Humevo. I looked at Jackson and he looked back at me. We both smiled. The silence between us was not at all uncomfortable.

Finally I spoke. "I would love to hear how you know José Humevo."

Jackson looked at me and shook his head ever so slightly. "Surely you know that I am not at liberty to share that information with you."

"What do you mean?"

I don't know if Jackson noticed the change of expression on my face, but I certainly noticed the change on his. He leaned forward. There was a tension in the air between us.

"Do you really know José Humevo?"

"Of course I do." My voice sounded defensive.

"But are you in training with him?"

"Not exactly. We met, he talked, I listened, and then he disappeared. Why are you questioning me like this?"

Jackson's face softened. He leaned back in his chair and smiled.

"I'm sorry, it's been so long that I'd forgotten what José Humevo told me about you." He started to laugh. "He kind of blew you out of the water, didn't he?"

I wasn't exactly sure what he was referring to. Jackson responded to the confusion on my face and laughed even louder. He held up his hand.

"Please forgive me, I am not laughing at you. I was merely remembering the way José Humevo told me the story about pouring too much information into this attentive young man before realizing that he had gone too far. He said that you were so receptive that he just kept going. When he saw that he had overloaded your system, he felt that the best thing to do was simply to leave you alone. He felt bad about disappearing the way he did, but he didn't know what else to do. We all make mistakes, even José Humevo. Mistakes are an integral part of the learning process."

Jackson's eyes were still smiling even though his laughter had subsided.

"I think it would be best if you read the letter before we continue. I cannot tell you any more about José Humevo at this time. If you'd like to talk with me later, you know where to find me."

"But..."

"Nils, I cannot help you any further until you understand the ground rules. Now, if you'll excuse me, I need to get ready for my next appointment."

Bing, bang, boom. Just like that I was standing outside of Jackson's office, no wiser than when I went in. I shuffled down the hallway, through the door that opened onto Red Square, and headed for the bench. It seemed like the appropriate place to read the letter. I sat down, turned the crumpled envelope over a couple of times in my hand before I tore off the end and pulled out the single sheet of paper. I unfolded the hand written note and began to read:

Nils,

I hope that this letter finds its way into your hands. I am leaving it with my good friend and fellow traveler, Jackson Barnes. If it is meant to be, you will find one another. Something came up that required my immediate attention. I apologize for any confusion my hasty departure may have caused you. My offer to share the principles of learning still stands.

I invite you to consider whether or not you are ready to begin this training. The journey is not easy, but there are many rewards along the way. I cannot overstate the importance of making this decision consciously, independently, and without hurry.

My only requirement is that our time together remains a private affair. The information I am sharing is not for public consumption at this time. This requirement is not negotiable. If your decision is no, there is nothing you need to do. If your decision is yes, contact Jackson and let him know that you are ready to begin. He will provide your next instructions. Take your time with this and use something other than your mind to decide.

– José Humevo

CLEAR INTENTIONS

◆

I SPENT THE next few days convincing myself why it would be a good idea to begin training with José Humevo. As soon as I made this decision, I began to encounter all the reasons why it would be a good idea to turn and run like hell from this mysterious man whom I barely knew. Each argument seemed equally reasonable at the time. So much so, that I was able to convince myself over and over again why one or the other decision was the best path to follow.

This tug-o-war went back and forth so many times that I had smoke coming out of my ears. It wasn't until I reached this mental meltdown that I focused on the last sentence of the letter, "Use something other than your mind to decide." Like what? My emotions, my intuition, my Ouija Board?

I had never owned a Ouija Board, but my friend

Gigi had one. We had played with it several times with less than clear results, but I was ready to grasp at any straw that I could find. I couldn't ask the question directly because I was committed to honor the request for privacy, so I asked for some clarity regarding my next steps. The Ouija Board spelled out a response: *Nils listens to wind, Gigi listens to sun.*

I looked at Gigi to see if the message made more sense to her than it did to me. She shrugged her shoulders. "What does that mean?"

The board did not respond. Gigi tried again. "Tell us more."

The communication was brief: *follow your heart.*

A flush of embarrassment darkened my face. The message had hit its target. I had not forgotten that I was supposed to figure this out on my own. My old pattern of trying to find the easy way out was not going to work this time. The message stopped Gigi in her tracks as well. It was clear that our session was over. She closed the Ouija Board and made a pot of tea. We changed the subject.

Halloween came and went and still I could not decide. I had seen Jackson a couple of times on campus but he would not engage with me beyond greetings and small talk. The door would not open by itself. The days and weeks rolled by.

I invited Tammy to join me for Thanksgiving at my parent's house. We went skiing the following day at Mount Baker with my brother Alan. On my third run down the mountain I found the answer I had been looking for. The answer was not in my head; it was in my body. My body knew how to ski quite independently from my mind. It would move or lean or adjust long before my mind could figure out what to do. All I had to do was relax, get out of the way, and let my body do what it knew how to do. If it worked while speeding down a steep snow-covered slope, why wouldn't it work at slower speeds as well?

My mind questioned if José Humevo was somehow trying to take advantage of me. My body knew that that was a Fantasized Experience Appearing Real. As soon as I stopped to feel into it, the answer became crystal clear. My body knew that I could trust José Humevo and wanted to be in his presence once again. He had nudged me outside my comfort zone, but there was no malice in him. He was what he said he was, a learning guide, someone who could help me find my way.

I went looking for Jackson as soon as I got back to Evergreen, but it took me a few days to catch up with him. I found him in his office mid-week, entered with a sense of conviction, and blurted out that I had decided to begin the training.

Jackson looked up from behind his desk and smiled. "What took you so long?" He reached behind his desk chair, grabbed a red delicious apple, and tossed it to me. "Eat this, you are about to begin your journey." He looked out the window. "Actually, you started the journey the moment you first crossed paths with José Humevo. You are now beginning the next phase."

I bit into the apple. It was fresh, crisp, and sweet. "What's next?" I asked, chewing on the apple, attempting to appear nonchalant.

Jackson pulled out an envelope from his desk drawer, opened it and began to read.

"Your assignment is to walk on the earth without shoes for at least twenty minutes a day for twenty-eight days in a row. If you miss a day at any time during the process, you are to begin at day one and continue until you have successfully completed twenty-eight consecutive days. It is important that you walk on native ground – a forest trail, a meadow, the beach – never on concrete or asphalt. These are dead surfaces that will drain, rather than enhance, your energy. A lawn will do in a pinch, but it is not ideal. The more natural the surface, the better. When you have successfully completed this assignment, return for your next set of instructions."

Jackson put down the paper and began to chuckle.

"That's it?" I asked.

Jackson shook his head almost imperceptibly. "Do not judge what you do not understand." Then he began to laugh.

"What's so funny?"

"I find it hilarious that this particular message is being delivered to you via a man with no toes." He wiped a tear of laughter from his eye. "José Humevo loves irony. I'm sure he did this on purpose."

"You mean it's a joke?"

"Oh, heavens no, this is no joke. There is humor in this communication, but he is deadly serious about the assignment."

"So, I'm supposed to walk barefoot for twenty minutes a day for twenty-eight days?"

"Precisely. It must be twenty-eight consecutive days, and remember that all of your dealings with José Humevo are to remain a private affair. You may share what you are doing but not why or with whom you are doing it. Is there anything about these instructions that you do not understand?"

"No. How could I tell anyone why I am walking barefoot when I don't understand it myself?"

"Understanding follows experience, not the other way around. Complete the assignment before expecting the payoff. Follow the instruction, stay open, and notice what you notice. This is how we learn and grow."

I left Jackson's office feeling less than exuberant, walked out to Red Square and sat on the bench that had become my home away from home. What in the world does walking barefoot have to do with anything? Were these guys having a bit of fun at my expense or was there really something to this barefoot thing? There was only one way to find out.

I walked to the grassy meadow behind the library, took off my shoes, and began. The grass, wet from the morning dew was surprisingly cold beneath my feet. I moved faster than normal at first, but as I slowed down the texture of the grass felt almost soothing. My toes began to spread out and push with more firmness and control. I wandered around in circles behind the library for about five minutes before approaching the trail to the beach.

I stashed my shoes behind a tree and stepped onto the trail. The bare soil was not as cushy as the meadow, but it was noticeably warmer. I enjoyed the feeling of moving slowly and quietly through the forest. My bare feet did not make as much noise as shoes and I began to see how quietly I could move. I was so busy practicing my stealth walk that I didn't notice the service road until it was under my feet. I don't know if it was the power of suggestion or what, but as soon as I stepped onto the asphalt it felt very unnatural. It lacked variation and texture. It actually did feel dead compared to the dirt or the grass.

I scampered across the road anxious to return to native soil. I stepped onto the trail expecting to feel the relative warmth and softness of the dirt. I was surprised when I felt a stinging sensation on the bottoms of my feet. I looked at the trail. Some genius had decided that it would be a good idea to cover this portion with crushed rock. I took a few more steps but it was not a barefoot-friendly surface. I turned around and let out a sigh when my feet made contact with the soft dirt. I returned to the meadow, the dampness now a welcome relief, and stayed there until my twenty minutes were up.

My feet were wet, dirty, and curiously energized. They did not go willingly back into my shoes. As I headed to Red Square, I was surprisingly aware of how my body moved. Maybe there was more to this assignment than I thought.

Over the next few days I continued to fine-tune my practice. I discovered a couple of other trail systems on campus and found a different route to the water where the trail had not been enhanced with crushed rock. I was especially glad to find this trail to the beach. I loved to walk along the shoreline, to listen to the seagulls and the crows calling out to one another. Eld Inlet felt expansive in juxta-position to the womb-like feeling of the forest.

The beach was a mixture of sand and small round pea gravel. It was a stimulating, yet pleasant surface to walk on. The trail to the beach was close to Red Square and took about twenty minutes to walk. It became my route of choice.

I discovered that carrying a bandana with me was a good idea. Being able to brush the dirt off my feet and dry them made the transition back to shoes and socks more enjoyable. After a week of either hiding or carrying my shoes I started wearing sandals. I found that I could strap them to the back of my fanny pack and take them with me. Also, going from no shoes to sandals felt more natural than strapping on boots or shoes after having my feet exposed to the elements.

The more I walked barefoot, the more my feet enjoyed it. Pretty soon I had parked my boots and shoes and wore sandals most of the time. I found that if my upper body was warm, it was not uncomfortable to have my feet exposed. People would look at me on chilly or rainy days like I was crazy, but it was no big deal. I remembered Jackson's words of advice – do not judge what you do not understand. I was experiencing increased freedom and awareness by exposing my feet and was not about to let a few strange looks stop my exploration.

I passed day fourteen, the halfway mark, during the last week of Fall Quarter. I wrote my evaluations, met with my professors, and walked barefoot to the beach every day. I stopped in to see Jackson to give him an update. He listened to my report, told me to keep up the good work, and then excused himself. He was busy with other students.

The quarter came to an end and I headed home for the holidays. My friends gave me a hard time about wearing sandals in December. My parents just shook their heads. It made me realize that my life at Evergreen was not entirely in sync with my life in Stanwood. I watched myself make subtle adjustments in my behavior in order to fit in. When in Rome.

On Christmas Eve day I went skiing with my brother. We left early in the morning, arriving at Stevens Pass just as the lifts opened. There was a foot of fresh powder snow and we hooted and hollered as we schussed the slopes. Powder in the Cascades is a rare treat, so even though we began to tire as the day worn on we kept doing one more run, again and again and again, until our legs were like jelly. Finally, we called it a day, loaded up our skis, and headed for home. The journey took longer than we had planned.

Snowplows were working overtime but they could not keep up with the storm. The highway was thick with snow and we had to chain up just to get out of the parking lot. It was slow going until we reached the lowlands and we arrived in Stanwood much later than expected. Olga was not happy. Dinner had been on the table for over an hour and there were presents to open and traditions to observe.

After several hours of festivities, holiday food, Scandinavian deserts, eggnog, and wine, I was ready to call it a day. My body was feeling the effects of too much food, alcohol, and exercise. I wandered off to my old bedroom and fell into a deep sleep.

As the sun came up I crawled out of bed and went looking for a cup of coffee. My body felt similar to the morning after my first day of peeling logs. Olga's black brew got me up and moving. I stepped outside to get the morning paper and as soon as my feet hit the ground I felt a pit in my stomach.

"I forgot to walk barefoot yesterday." I hit myself on the head. "Fuck, fuck, fuck! I was on day twenty-four. I was almost done. What an idiot." I couldn't believe the oversight. I was so close. The change in my daily pattern had thrown me off. I was so sure of success that I had lost my focus.

Olga demonstrated the power of motherly intuition by asking me what was wrong as soon as I walked back into the house.

"Nothing. I just realized that I forgot to do something."

"Can I help?"

"No, I need to take care of it myself."

She started to speak again, but then stopped herself, gave me a quick hug and let me be. I wondered off with a scowl on my face, silently beating myself up while everyone around me was engaged in Christmas cheer. After moping around the house for a couple of hours I drove to a waterfront park near my parents' home that I used to frequent during my high school days. It was a place where I could be alone in nature, to reflect and to ponder. I always went there by myself, never with friends. It was a place where I found balance in the topsy-turvy world of adolescence.

As I looked out to the water I remembered the words of advice that Jackson had shared with me. "Mistakes are an integral part of the learning process." I tried to ignore the memory but it wouldn't go away.

Eventually I accepted what had happened. It wasn't as if the last twenty-four days were a complete waste of time. I had received value from my barefoot walking and dropping the ball was another lesson along the way. I took off my sandals and walked the trail to the beach. After twenty minutes I felt more centered, balanced, and whole. I had begun the process again, this time with a clear intention to see it all the way through to the end. Day one complete, twenty-seven days to go.

SHIFT IN PERCEPTION

◆

I RETURNED TO Olympia the day after Christmas and settled into my new routine. I decided that walking first thing in the morning was the best way for me to insure a successful twenty-eight day practice. Tammy had gone away for the holidays and I had the house to myself. I would get up every morning, drive to campus, take off my shoes and begin walking. Sometimes I would walk for twenty minutes, sometimes longer. My feet had seasoned over time. They were much less sensitive than they were when I first started out.

On New Year's Day I wanted to do something different, so I decided to walk the crushed rock path to the beach. I had been avoiding that route since my initial encounter with it. I was surprised to find that my memory of the trail was no longer accurate. I discovered that the sharpness of the crushed rock dissipated to the degree that I was able to relax into it. The path that I had been avoiding had much to teach me about my old patterns, beliefs, and assumptions. I began to wonder where else I was allowing outdated beliefs to influence my choices.

I walked that trail every day for the next week. By the time Tammy returned I was ten days into my renewed practice. A few days later I ran into Jackson in the gym and told him about missing day twenty-four and starting over with new resolve.

"It sounds like it has been a valuable experience, Nils. Stay with it."

Jackson's words gave me an added boost. I was halfway to my goal and feeling confident. The next morning I woke up to six inches of snow on the ground. I stared out the kitchen window at the winter wonderland outside, half of me appreciating the beauty of the snow that had fallen during the night, half of me wondering how I was going to walk barefoot under these conditions.

Olympia, like all the cities and towns in the lowlands of Puget Sound, was not accustomed to snow. It was an infrequent occurrence that wreaked havoc with transportation systems and schools. Classes at Evergreen were cancelled. Tammy got up and was bouncing off the walls like a schoolgirl. She wanted to go outside and make a snowman.

"Don't you mean a snow person?"

"Snow person this."

Tammy flipped me off and smiled. The kid in me wanted to go out and play, but the responsible adult wanted to take care of my commitments first. I knew what the task was, I just wasn't sure how I was going to accomplish it. Three cups of coffee later it was clear that I was fully engaged in avoidance behavior.

Tammy finally convinced me to join her on the front lawn. Her enthusiasm was contagious and eventually wore me down. As soon as we started rolling balls of snow, I really got into it. We made a giant snowman and adorned it with a hat, scarf, and carrot nose. We laughed a lot in the process.

Snow girl went inside to make hot chocolate while I stayed to admire our creation. As I stood back I noticed the patches of grass that we had exposed while rolling balls of snow. We had created a snow-free labyrinth on the lawn. I touched the freshly exposed grass, it was considerably warmer than the snow. A light bulb went off inside my head.

My original instructions stated that a lawn would do in a pinch. I considered this just such a moment. I took off my shoes, looked at my watch, and started following the path we had created. The grass was cold, but not unbearable. I smiled and kept walking. I had completed a couple of laps around the front yard when Tammy came outside with a cup of hot chocolate. She stood on the porch shaking her head.

"What the hell are you doing?"

I put on my best New York accent. "I'm walkin' here."

"I can see that, Einstein. Why are you barefoot?"

"I don't know, I just wanted to see how it felt.

Would you like to join me?"

"Uh...no thanks. Would you like this hot chocolate now or after your feet turn blue?"

"Now." I ran over to the front porch and took the cup from her hand. "Thanks."

Tammy shook her head again and went back inside. I held the warm cup in both hands and got back on my mini trail system. I had crossed undisturbed snow on my way to the porch and now my feet were beginning to sting. My toes got colder and colder as the minutes eked by. The more I looked at my watch, the slower it seemed to move.

With ten minutes to go, I knew I needed a distraction. For some reason I started singing every Neil Young song I could remember. After awhile I added the air guitar and really got into it. Tammy returned to the porch to see what the commotion was all about.

"Did you eat some magic mushrooms this morning?"

"No, but thanks for asking. Can I have some more hot chocolate?"

Tammy rolled her eyes. "Bring me your cup."

I headed for the porch, but this time I stayed on the path. By the time my second cup of hot chocolate arrived, I had less than five minutes to go. It was the longest five minutes of my life and it took everything I had to make it to the finish line. Finally, my twenty minutes were up and I scampered into the house. My feet were not blue, but they were mighty red.

"You just about done with your little adventure there, Huckleberry?"

"Why yes I are, widow Douglas. You don't know where a fella could get cleaned up do ya?"

Tammy chased me into the bathroom. I got there first and locked the door behind me. "Don't you come out of there until those feet are presentable, young man."

"Yes, Ma'am."

I tended to my semi-frozen feet while sitting on the edge of the bathtub. I started with cold water and slowly increased the temperature to cool and then to lukewarm. I knew that I needed to take my time with this. As I was waiting for the feeling to return to my toes, I thought about how unexpectedly my morning had unfolded. If Tammy hadn't kept encouraging me to play, I would have been up on campus slogging through the snow in my bare feet, all in the name of being responsible. I probably would have gotten frostbite if I had followed the "should" voice going off inside my head. It was in allowing myself to have a little fun that a better solution appeared. Once again I caught a glimpse of one of the old habits that was keeping me more constricted than I had realized. When would I ever learn?

My toes came back to life, I dried my feet, rubbed them with lotion and put on a fresh pair of wool socks. Tammy wanted to play some more. I watched as I started to hesitate, caught myself, and laughed as I agreed to join her outside. Old habits are persistent if nothing else. The day was still young and I decided to simply allow it to unfold. This time, however, I put on my boots before leaving the house.

That night rain returned to Western Washington and melted the snow. In the morning, our snowman was still standing but the rest of the white stuff had disappeared. Life was back to normal and I returned to my morning routine of walking the trail to the beach. I was at the halfway point, but this time I wasn't feeling so cocky. The snow walk had pushed me to my limit and I wasn't taking anything for granted from here on out. I kept my head down and focused on my practice, one day at a time.

When I looked up it was the morning of day twenty-eight. I savored the experience, spending some extra time down at the beach, writing in my journal and thinking about the day that I had first walked that same trail with José Humevo. I wondered where he was and what my next assignment would be.

I was proud of what I had accomplished. It had been a bigger task than I had originally thought. I didn't have a clue what I was getting myself into when I agreed to take this on. It seemed rather pointless to me at the time. I would never have guessed that I could learn so much about myself simply by walking barefoot on the earth for twenty-eight consecutive days.

I stopped by Jackson's office when I returned from the beach but he was not there. I was feeling energized, so I headed over to the gym to see if I could pick up a quick game of racquetball. I walked by the courts to see if anyone was looking for a partner and saw Jackson in his boxer shorts playing a student who was half his age. I watched for awhile through the small window in the door. Jackson was the one in his underwear, but he was clearly beating the pants off his opponent. I shook my head and laughed.

My buddy, Chuck, saw me laughing and came over

to see what was so funny. We peered through the window together. The longer we watched the further Jackson increased his lead. His movements were not particularly graceful, but they were certainly effective. The outcome of the game did not appear to be in doubt. Chuck invited me to join him in the adjoining court. After forty-five minutes my tee shirt was dripping and I was ready for a shower. Jackson was long gone by the time I got dressed.

I checked his office one more time and came up empty handed again. I had been excited to share my accomplishment with him, but it felt like the moment had passed. I was disappointed as I walked to the parking lot. By the time I got to my car, I started to admit to myself that I had been looking for external acknowledgement to validate what I already felt inside myself. This need for the approval of others was an old pattern that was holding me back from being my full self. I had figured this out intellectually a long time ago, but somehow my emotional body couldn't or wouldn't let it go.

It took three days for me to catch up with Jackson. He seemed genuinely pleased when I told him that I had completed my assignment. However, he was mysteriously vague when I asked him what was next. He told me that I could continue the practice or not, that it was my choice, and that he would get back to me. He seemed preoccupied and raced off in the middle of the conversation.

A week later I still hadn't heard a thing. I walked every day, but the passion was slipping away. There was something wrong that I couldn't quite name. Then it came to me. I was operating more out of habit than intention. As soon as I was able to verbalize it, I could see that it was simply a variation of the same old pattern. The good boy inside of me wanted to please, to do it right, to excel. If twenty-eight days was good, then thirty-eight was better, forty-eight better still. I was going through the motions, checking the boxes on my list of things to do.

The next morning I made a decision to stop walking barefoot. I felt guilty all day long and had to restrain myself from heading to the beach. Every time I got the urge, I stopped to tune in. It always felt like an obligation instead of a genuine desire. I was tired of my predictable knee-jerk response to try to meet the perceived expectations of others.

I had been programmed to do what was right, whatever the hell that was. I had developed a liberal, free-spirited facade to counteract the deep sense of duty that had been passed on to me by Albert and Olga. They, of course, had learned it from their parents, who had learned it from their parents, who had learned it from their parents. On and on, down through the generations, this pattern had been passed along. Now it was mine to have and to hold. I had been denying this fact since the onset of adolescence and had created an elaborate matrix of smoke screens and mirrors to reinforce the story that I kept telling myself. I am not like them. I am fluid, flexible, and free. This was my mantra, but underneath my long hair and beard I was holding myself more tightly than I had realized.

One of the reasons that the Evergreen womyn had irritated me so much was because they had been a mirror for me, liberal on the outside and constricted within. Their controlling nature bled through their politically correct attitudes and it drove me crazy.

My grandmother used to tell me that when one finger is pointing outward, there are three fingers pointing back. I hadn't fully understood her point until that very moment. Passing judgement on others says as much, if not more, about the person pointing than it does about those being pointed at. People who are sure that they know the best way or the only way are usually the ones who are lost. They lose track of where they are because they confuse the map of the terrain with the terrain itself.

It does not work to lay a rigid belief system over the undulating contours of a human life and expect everything to fall into neat little boxes. I understood how ineffective this was for everyone else – I had been pointing my finger at them for years. It had never occurred to me that I might be in the same boat. I had been so busy trying to avoid this, that, or the other pitfall, that I had not noticed the tangled web I had been weaving around myself.

The problem was not out there, and neither was the solution. There was no right way to be, other than to be authentically me. I had spent so much of my life trying to *do it right* that I had lost sight of my true nature. I had become so preoccupied with receiving external feedback that somewhere along the way I had stopped listening to my own internal guidance system. The map I had been using was not entirely accurate. No wonder I felt lost.

When I got home that night, the first thing I did was take off my shoes and walk barefoot on the lawn. My feet had become accustomed to direct contact with the earth and they wanted to feel that connection again. I didn't care that it was the front lawn and not the forest. I didn't care that it was ten minutes instead of twenty. I simply did what my body wanted to do and I didn't care what anyone else thought, not Tammy, not Jackson, not even José Humevo. This connection to the earth beneath my feet was for me and me alone.

As I strolled around the front yard, the clouds opened up to reveal the beauty and the splendor of the night sky. I noticed the wide spectrum of color emanating from the stars – blue, red, green, yellow. Stars had always seemed more or less white to me before. The longer I looked the more I realized that I was looking out into, rather than up at, the stars that surround the earth. This subtle shift in perception completely changed my understanding of the universe. Standing outside in suburban West Side Olympia, bare feet on the ground and wide eyes scanning the cosmos, I felt about as connected to the world around me, and to myself, as I ever had.

I walked inside the house and found a note pinned to my bedroom door: Meet Jackson Barnes at the Art Deco Diner tomorrow at noon for lunch. I shook my head. It had been quite a day.

CHOICE POINT

———————◆———————

THE ART DECO was a famous eating establishment in Olympia. It was a gathering spot for hippies and loggers, students and professors, politicians and blue-collar workers. The two gray-haired women who prepared the food created an atmosphere that cut across all social-political boundaries. It was a place of healing in the most basic sense of the word. Whenever I needed a pick-me-up I headed for the Art Deco.

My favorite meal was the soup, salad, and bread special. The soup was healthy, hearty, and home-made, the salad was simple and green, and the bread was fresh out of the oven, two inches thick, and grilled on the stove top, if you requested. I always requested. Normally, I would follow this with a hand scooped milkshake made in a stainless steel container that filled the tall fountain glass two times or more. I liked the Art Deco.

I walked inside, took in the smell of fresh baked bread, and looked around. Jackson was in the booth next to the far wall. He was facing me, engaged in a conversation with someone I could not see. I didn't know we were going to have another guest. As I approach the booth, the person across from Jackson turned and smiled.

"Hola, mi amigo."

My body jerked involuntarily as José Humevo and Jackson Barnes burst into laughter. They jumped up, patted me on the back, and quickly sat back down next to one another on the side where Jackson had been sitting. They simultaneously gestured for me to sit facing them. I sat down, my head still spinning from the surprise. Their weathered faces and wrinkled eyes exaggerated their humorous expressions. They looked like a couple of mischievous schoolboys laughing and telling jokes with the waitress as she attempted to take our order. They didn't settle down until she returned with our food and we began to eat.

José Humevo spoke first. "Please share with us the awareness you have gained from your barefoot walking practice."

The sudden change in mood took me by surprise. So did the question. It took me a moment to find a place to begin. I told them about my indecision around whether or not to start the training, about tuning into my body for the answer, and about my initial disappointment with the assignment.

"Quite frankly, I was expecting something a bit

more esoteric."

They smiled in unison. When I told them about my suspicions that they were playing games with me, the laughter started again.

I talked about my surprise at how freeing it felt to walk barefoot and how I began to fine-tune the process as I went along. I shared my first impressions of the crushed rock and the assumptions that I made based on that experience. I told them about losing my focus and missing day twenty-four and how I beat myself up about it before starting over with new resolve.

When I shared the story about the snow day, they were beside themselves. Jackson howled with laughter when I explained the part about singing and playing the air guitar. They both nodded when I talked about the realizations I had about my patterns around responsibility and obligation.

I admitted to my dependence on positive feedback and my disappointment and confusion when Jackson seemed distant and noncommittal towards the process once I had completed the twenty-eight days. I told them how his response had highlighted my understanding of how I had been trying to meet the perceived expectations of others for far too many years.

Finally, I shared my awareness that I had somehow lost contact with my inner voice, and the small success I had had the night before, walking barefoot on the lawn and gazing at the stars for no reason other than that was what I wanted to do.

The two of them stared at me for a long time after I

had finished. José Humevo finally broke the silence.

"That was an excellent recounting of your experience." He turned to Jackson and touched him on the shoulder. "This man has been your gatekeeper and only he may let you pass. What say you old wise one?"

Jackson continued to stare at me, his head nodding very slowly. "Let the young man pass. He has earned the right."

His words triggered something inside of me and my eyes began to fill with tears. There was playfulness in their manner and yet they seemed extremely serious at the same time.

"You must thank the gatekeeper for his time. His task is complete."

"How do I do that?"

There was a pause as they turned to look at one another. "Shake his hand and buy his lunch. We are simple men."

"Done," I said, reaching my arm across the table. Jackson took my hand and gave it a firm squeeze.

"I am sure you will travel far. I now turn you over to the capable hands of José Humevo. I must be on my way. Thank you for lunch."

"My pleasure," I called out as he made his way to the door.

"That is one amazing human being," José Humevo said. "You have been very fortunate to have had him as your gatekeeper. More than you may ever know."

José Humevo and I left the Art Deco shortly after Jackson's departure and drove to campus. He wanted to return to the spot on the beach where we had parted ways. There was an awkward silence between us. We did not yet share the same ease that he and Jackson seemed to have together.

We walked across Red Square, around to the back of the library, and entered the trailhead to the beach. We kept our shoes on and walked in silence through the forest. I noticed the thick moss hanging from the alder trees and giant maples, the fresh smell of the air, the color and texture of the decomposing leaves on the forest floor. I heard the distinct call of a pileated woodpecker as we hiked toward Eld Inlet.

When we got to the beach José Humevo sat down with his back against a driftwood log. I joined him and we sat quietly for a few minutes. The low-lying fog hanging over the water was soft and peaceful. His words caught me off guard as they broke the silence.

"I am not a shaman, a guru, or a priest. I am a human being whose life is in the process of unfolding. I do what I can to help it along. I am a learning guide and I am offering to help you become a more fully developed human being.

"The word education comes from the Latin *educare*, which means to draw forth from within. Education is not about pouring information into an empty vessel. It is about awakening the awareness, understanding, and knowledge that lies dormant within us all. I have developed some relatively simple principles and practices that can assist this awakening. This is what I offer. All I ask in return is your agreement to keep our relationship private and your commitment to pass this information on to others when the time is right."

"How will I know when the time is right?"

"You will know."

"But what if I don't know?"

"If you do not know, then I have not completed my half of the agreement and you will be free from further obligation. Is this acceptable to you?"

"Yes."

"The barefoot walking practice you completed offered a glimpse into the awareness and understanding that is available to you. You seemed to have received value from that experience. Would you like to officially begin your training at this time?"

"Yes, I would."

"Then you must ask me to be your guide."

"I would like you to be my guide."

"That is a statement, not a request. You have given me nothing to respond to. Precise language is important." He wagged his finger at me. "Try again."

"I am consciously choosing to begin the training at this time. Will you be my guide?"

"Do you fully understand the commitment you are making?"

"Yes."

"Tell me what that commitment is."

"If I enter into this training my commitment is to keep the details of our relationship private and to pass along that which I learn when the time is right."

"Is there anything about this commitment that you

do not understand or do not agree with?"

"No."

"Then I agree to be your guide." José Humevo picked up a stick and drew a line in the sand. "If you agree to all that we have carefully and consciously stated to one another, then stand up and step across this line. When you step across this line, we will have made a contract and the training will officially begin. It is of utmost importance that you take this step consciously and of your own free will. The choice must come from within you. Take whatever time you need."

José Humevo had a strange effect on my moods. I felt alert, curious, cautious, and frightened, all at the same time. What had seemed like a simple decision a few moments earlier now held much more weight. I looked at the line in the sand. It was a line in the sand, and yet it was more than that. I thought I had made this decision the day I walked into Jackson's office and announced that I was ready to begin. I thought I had made it just a minute ago. Now I was being asked to make the decision a third time.

Why was he being so precise about this? What was I missing? Was there a piece that I did not understand? Suddenly, all my doubts and demons came rushing to the surface. I looked at José Humevo; he was staring at the water as if I was not even there. I didn't want to play this game. I stood up and started to step across the line, but something inside of me put on the brakes. I growled involuntarily. José Humevo sat there, not moving, not looking at me, not saying a word. I fell into an internal debate.

It's just a line in the sand.

No, it is a choice point.
I've already made this choice.
Really?
Yes, twice before.
Then why do you still have doubts?
I don't have doubts!
Then why don't you step across the line?

I looked at the line again, and as I did, my body began to shake. I couldn't move forward and I couldn't stand still. I turned and began to walk in the opposite direction. The movement eased the pressure that had been building up inside of me. I walked about fifty feet and stopped, turned back and looked at José Humevo. Part of me hoped that he might not be there so that I wouldn't have to deal with him. He hadn't moved and he didn't appear to be going anywhere anytime soon.

I turned my back to him and kept walking until I knew I was out of his line of sight. I wanted to be alone. It was so ironic. The first time we were on the beach he disappeared when I wanted him to stay. Now he wouldn't leave when part of me wanted him to go away. Who was this guy? Why was he pressing me to commit? What did he want? Could he really be trusted?

The questions kept coming, and as they did I found myself walking faster and faster. My breathing was shallow, my neck was tense. A crow swooped down from a nearby tree and splattered a huge bird poop on my right sandal.

"Damn it!" I shook my fist at the crow who cackled back at me as it disappeared into the fog. I stormed over to the water's edge, took off my sandal, and rinsed my foot in

Eld Inlet. I scraped the white goo off the top of my sandal and swished it in the water. I was about to put my sandal back on when I realized how refreshing the water felt on my foot. I took off my other sandal, clipped the pair to the back of my fanny pack, and eased both feet into the cool water.

My breathing started to slow down and deepen. The tension in my neck began to relax. I rolled my pant legs to my knees and waded in deeper. The water was soothing. As I walked, my shoulders softened, my jaw dropped, and my mind quieted down. I strolled along, relaxing more and more with every step. I watched my feet as they moved in and out of the water, noticed the tiny wake created by my ankles as they pushed forward, felt my toes gripping the sand. I breathed in the salt air. The lowness of the fog and the narrowness of the inlet created a womb-like feeling. What in the world had I been so upset about? Why did I blow up like that?

I looked up and noticed José Humevo in the distance, still sitting on the same spot, still looking straight ahead. I had the feeling that he could sit there for days if he had to. I stepped out of the water and moved in a straight line directly towards him. I walked up to the line and stepped over it without breaking my stride. There was no hesitation or doubt in my movement. It was a clear, concise, conscious action. It felt incredibly liberating.

I looked at José Humevo; he was still gazing out at the water. I had a brief moment of confusion and then my body sat down beside him of its own volition. I leaned my back against the log and waited. His head began to nod, almost imperceptibly and then he turned and looked me in the eye. It was the same look that he had given me on the day when we first met. He scanned my body and then met my eyes again. His gaze softened and he turned his head back towards the water.

"My name is José Humevo and I am an evolutionary. I am committed to supporting the evolution of human awareness, understanding, and knowledge. By consciously stepping over the line you have joined me in this endeavor. Your body, your mind, and your spirit were aware of the seriousness and commitment involved in performing this conscious act. This is not the first time we have had this conversation.

"The last time we sat on this spot I made the same offer to you. I mistook your natural level of receptivity as a willingness and an ability to consciously choose to move forward. I gave you too much information at that time, and even though your body and your spirit wanted more, your mind seized up. You actually lost consciousness for a short period of time and I realized that I had gone too far. As soon as I was certain that you were going to be all right, I decided to slip away. I did not know how much you would remember and I figured that it would be easier for your mind if I simply disappeared.

"I apologize for any confusion this may have caused you. The way your mind reacted took me by surprise and I handled it the best way I could. The experience of being a conscious human being is a practice; all we can do is do the best we can. I can be embarrassed by my shortcomings and attempt to hide them from others, or I can embrace my mistakes and learn to fail forward. Mistakes are an integral part of the learning process. This is the third *principle of learning*.

"This afternoon, your body, your mind, and your spirit began to remember our initial conversation. I deliberately brought you back to this spot because I suspected that it would reawaken the part of you that has been lying dormant. Your body and your spirit woke up quite easily but your mind refused to budge. I had to tease it out of its slumber. As it started to wake up, your mind sensed the memory of the overload that you experienced last time and it went into a defensive mode of operation. This is all very understandable. I imagine that you had an interesting internal struggle. There was nothing I could do for you. You had to follow the process through to the end.

"I knew your body would eventually take charge and calm your mind and that your spirit would lead you back to choice point. I was relatively certain that you were going to cross the line, but there was the possibility that you would not. We always have free choice. That is something that can never be taken away.

"You were fully aware that you were at choice point. It was up to you to decide if you were going to move forward or not. Had you decided to decline the offer, our time together would have come to an end. You chose to step forward and as a result of that action our journey now moves to the next level. Everything up to this point has been initiation and warm up."

José Humevo reached out his hand, touched my shoulder, and looked me directly in the eye.

87

"Welcome, little brother, I am pleased that you have joined us."

His words swirled around my head, lifting a veil from my eyes. It reminded me of the shift in awareness that occurred while I was looking at the stars the night before. I caught a glimpse of the possibilities available to me in particular and to humanity in general. José Humevo interrupted my thoughts with a gentle chuckle that began in his midsection and slowly made its way to his mouth. I watched it ripple up his body and flow out of him completely without pretense, effort, or force. As far as I could tell, this was the way he lived his life.

His laughter echoed across Eld Inlet and slowly faded in the distance. There was a moment of silence before he spoke.

"The real training begins now."

MOON CYCLES

◆

"THE TWENTY-EIGHT DAY practice is the foundation of this training." With these words, José Humevo introduced me to Advanced Human Awareness – what he referred to as *aha!*

"The answers to life's questions are always within reach. It is simply a matter of knowing where and how to find them. Every person I know has experienced a moment when the answer to a question suddenly reveals itself, as if by magic. This is an *aha!* moment – an alignment with Advanced Human Awareness.

"Advanced Human Awareness is not a skill one learns in school. It is not found out there," he said, sweeping his hand in front of his body. "It is found in here." He touched the center of his chest. "Remember, education means to draw forth from within. It is the process of learning how to access the awareness, understanding, and knowledge that lives within our DNA, which I like to think of as Discover Now Again, the practice of bringing myself back into the moment, again and again.

"As I told you the first time when we were on this beach, it is not so much about learning as it is about unlearning. Humanity has developed some rather bizarre habits over the millennia. We have passed these behavioral patterns and habits from generation to generation for so long that we have come to accept them, without question, as the way things are. It is the unquestioned assumptions about the nature of the human experience that keep us locked into our limited understanding of ourselves and the world in which we live. The closer those assumptions are to our core, the harder they are to recognize. They are so much a part of our day to day experience that they become nearly invisible.

"The answers to the big questions of life are found in our DNA – Discover Now Again. The answers are revealed through the practice of coming fully present to this moment, right here and right now, over and over again. Advanced Human Awareness resides in the eternal now. Discovering how to live in the eternal now is the key to experiencing a life overflowing with *aha!* moments.

"The reason I say that there is nothing we have to learn in order to reach this level of awareness is because this is our natural state of being. It is our birthright. It is programmed into our DNA. Discover Now Again and you will be free – free from the layers of faulty opinions, beliefs, and assumptions that have been with us for so long that we have come to accept them as truth.

"This is a relatively simple concept but it is not necessarily an easy one to employ. Over the years we have been programmed to accept certain baseline assumptions as true. These "truths" are *patterns of being* that have been repeated so many times that they have become unquestioned habitual patterns for most humans. These patterns can be altered, but it requires focus, action, and resolve to complete the transformation. The simple part is choosing to replace a habitual pattern with a more conscious one. The challenging part is doing the work required, moment to moment, in order to keep the pattern from reasserting itself. This is where the twenty-eight day practice comes in.

"Am I consciously choosing my response in the moment, or am I unconsciously repeating a knee-jerk reaction based on habitual patterns from my past? This is the question I must ask myself over and over again. The answer to this question is the mantra, Discover Now Again. This is not a new concept. Mystics and sages have been saying the same thing for centuries. This awareness, understanding, and knowledge has been passed forward within small pockets of humanity from generation to generation. It is the counter point to the larger unconscious habitual patterns that have also traveled down through the ages.

"My intent as an evolutionary is to discover an effective way to communicate this ancient awareness in a manner that is understandable and applicable in this day and age. The way forward shifts under our feet as we learn and grow. We live in a dynamic universe that is constantly in motion. In order to ride the wave of cosmic consciousness that flows throughout infinity and eternity, we must remain fluid and flexible.

"Infinity is never ending space. Eternity is never ending time. It is one of the great paradoxes of consciousness that infinity and eternity are most readily experienced by learning how to come fully present to the here and now. It is the ability to remain in the here and now that opens the doorway to the magic, awe, and mystery of *All That Is*."

"*All That Is?*"

"Yes. What do you remember about *All That Is*?"

"I don't remember anything."

José Humevo quickly scanned my body. His eyes looked focused and distant at the same time. "That's enough for now. I explained *All That Is* to you the last time we were together. It may have been the point where your mind overloaded. We will continue this conversation later. We don't want a repeat performance of last time, now do we?" He winked and smiled. "Let's walk."

I started to ask a question as we stood up but he cut me off.

"There is nothing you have to do with this information, other than to allow it to seep into your body, your mind, and your spirit. Think of it as a cup of hot tea that is brewing. Allow it to steep for awhile before you enjoy it."

We walked along the shore of Eld Inlet. The tide had come in and there was only a small strip of dry land between the water and the thick vegetation that hung over the beach. My sandals were still tied to the back of my fanny pack and José Humevo encouraged me to wade into the water as we strolled along.

"It will help ground you."

As soon as he said this I realized how tired I was. I had been so focused on what he was saying that I had not noticed my fatigue. Stepping into the water produced the same results it had earlier in the day. After a short distance I felt more centered, balanced, and whole. The longer we walked the better I felt. I enjoyed the silence. I noticed baby salmon jumping near the shoreline. A pair of cormorants were diving underwater and popping up again and again. A small flock of mallard ducks passed by at low altitude, looking for a suitable place to land. My mind was relaxed, my body strong, my spirit energized. I could have walked for hours.

José Humevo stopped and faced me. "This is where we part company for now. You did a good job tracking all that I shared this afternoon. Allow this information to settle into your body, mind, and spirit. Invite it to align with your DNA as you begin to Discover Now Again. Walk until you sense that it is time to stop and then go home and rest. Meet me here tomorrow at sunset and we will continue."

José Humevo stepped onto a trail that I had not noticed before and disappeared into the forest. I watched him go without question or concern and continued on my way. I'm not sure how long I walked. I felt extremely alert and very much in the moment. At some point my body stopped and turned around. It was time to go home.

The next evening I was at the beach at 5:00. It was an hour before sunset and I was looking forward to some time alone outdoors. Daylight in the Pacific Northwest is in short supply in the wintertime. My day had been full of schoolwork and general life maintenance. I grabbed some-thing to eat at the deli on campus, ate it on the bench in Red Square, and walked barefoot to the beach.

The combination of finding José Humevo at the Art Deco, crossing the line in the sand, and attempting to absorb the rapid-fire explanation of his concepts had had a strange effect on me. I had been extremely focused while listening to José Humevo on the beach, surprisingly tired immediately afterwards, and re-energized while walking in the water. By the time I got home, my thinking was clear, my body rested, and my spirit...activated. I don't know how else to describe it. It was as if there were more of me present. It was an unusual feeling, but not an unpleasant one. However, it did take some getting used to. I thought the sensation might begin to fade but it stayed with me all night. I went to bed late and woke up early, full of energy. The feeling did not wane as my day unfolded.

When I got to the beach, I found a comfortable log to lean against and spent some time capturing my thoughts. My old self would have felt overwhelmed by all that had happened, but for some reason I went in a different direc-tion this time. I embraced my new feelings rather than try-ing to force them into old familiar boxes.

I sat on the beach, writing in my journal. The air began to cool as the sun touched the horizon. A paper-thin crescent moon appeared as daylight drained from the sky. The upper arc of the sun was about to disappear when I felt a hand touch my shoulder. I gasped involuntarily. The sound of my rapidly inhaling breath was overlapped by a soft rhythmic chuckle coming from behind me. José Humevo had arrived. My immediate impulse was to be irritated with him for startling me, but one look at his boyish grin softened my reaction and I began to laugh.

"Buenos tardes," he said.

I nodded my head. "Buenos tardes."

I don't know why, but José Humevo always greeted me in Spanish. It was the only time he did not use English. I supposed he might have said "adiós" when leaving, but the guy never bothered to say good-bye. His pattern of simply walking away when he was complete remained unchanged for the duration of our relationship.

He joined me on the beach and we sat in silence for a few minutes as was customary during our initial time together. He scanned my body. "How are you feeling?"

"I feel surprisingly energized and clear."

"Good. I am learning how to pace myself with you. What else do you notice?"

"I have felt centered all day long and..."

"No, what do you notice right now?"

"What do you mean?" The clarity I had been feeling all day began to slip through my fingers.

He repeated his words slowly, "What do you notice right now? What do you notice around you?" He swept his arm in front of him like he had the day before, and then turned to face me, his eyebrows raised.

"I'm noticing that you're freaking me out a little bit."

"That is an internal awareness and not important to the point I am attempting to make. What do you notice outside of yourself?" he said, sweeping his arm one more time.

"I notice the temperature dropping. I notice the movement of the water. I notice the color of the sky."

"And in the sky?"

"I notice the sliver of a new moon."

"Bingo!"

"Bingo?"

"Yes, bingo. The reason we are here is to witness the moon. Do you remember the very first thing I said to you yesterday as I explained Advanced Human Awareness?"

"Yes, you said that the twenty-eight day practice is the foundation of the training."

"And what does the moon have to do with the twenty-eight day practice?" He raised his eyebrows once again.

"The moon follows a twenty-eight day cycle?"

"Yes. The moon revolves around the earth every twenty-eight days. It is a twenty-eight day revolution. And what does revolution mean?" He stopped, spread his hands apart before answering his own question. "It means to change fundamentally or completely. The cycle of the moon is directly linked to Advanced Human Awareness."

José Humevo smiled his boyish grin. "And what do you get when you remove the 'R' from revolution? You get evolution. Revolution, evolution, the moon, *aha!* Advanced Human Awareness training is linked to the cycle of the moon. The twenty-eight day cycle is the foundation that supports this training.

"It is my belief that as a species we have lost our

way. The diversion from the evolutionary path has occurred so slowly that it is nearly imperceptible. The stumbling around that we have come to accept as normal human behavior is not the only way to be. There is another choice we can make. There is another way to be.

"The key to finding our way back to the evolutionary path lies in awareness. The first step is to stop moving in the direction we are going. The second step is to move backwards, in the direction from which we came. Sometimes the most effective way forward is accomplished by retreating.

"Women understand this better than men do. They are connected to the twenty-eight day cycle through their menstrual flow. It is a natural part of the female experience. Men have to raise their awareness in order to come into alignment with this rhythmic pattern. Western culture has turned away from honoring or even acknowledging this connection. We call people who are mesmerized by the moon, lunatics. We call sensitive boys sissies. We tell our young men to stuff their feelings, to toughen up, to be a man.

"We worship competition and idolize the winners in sports, politics, and business. This suppresses our willingness to celebrate the victories of anyone we view as a competitor. If you are winning, I must be losing – this is the prevailing attitude. It is an old, worn out paradigm that does not encourage us to move forward together. In order to move forward together, we have *to-get-her*. We have to understand and embrace the feminine in ways we have forgotten.

In order to do this we must remember, *re-member* – to put ourselves back together. We have to put ourselves back (step back) in order *to-get-her* (to understand the feminine).

"The old patriarchal *pattern of being* is dying. We can either release it gracefully or have it ripped from our ever-tightening grip. Balance will return one way or another. We cannot continue down the path we are on much longer. Most people sense this at their core even if they are unable to articulate it."

José Humevo proceeded to tell me the story of an experiment that was done with frogs. Several frogs were put into a large container of water that was heated on a burner, very slowly, one degree at a time. After three or four hours the water reached a temperature that was hot enough to boil the frogs alive. The fatal shift in temperature occurred so gradually that the frogs in the container did not respond to the danger. Their early warning systems kept adjusting to the subtle increases in temperature until it was too late.

Once all the frogs were dead, the heat was stabilized and their bodies were removed. Then a new frog was put into the container. As soon as it hit the water, the frog recognized the inhospitable nature of the environment and immediately jumped out. Several more frogs were placed in the container with the same results.

The frogs that were fresh to the hot water immediately sensed the danger and removed themselves from the life-threatening situation. The frogs that were heated over time lost that sense of danger, even though the water was exactly the same temperature.

"The water temperature is increasing for humanity. I am a fresh frog, here to wake you up, to bring you to your senses. The twenty-eight day practice will help you redis-cover the power of the moon, the feminine, the yin aspects of life. This is what I offer. This is what you stepped into when you consciously chose to cross the line in the sand.

"This journey is not easy, but there are many rewards along the way. You already know too much to return to your old patterns. The path forward is revealed through the process of dismantling the faulty assumptions that have permeated your worldview. The water you are in is not comfortably warm. It is dangerously hot and getting hotter all the time.

"The twenty-eight day practice is your ticket out of this precarious situation. The moon will be your guide. It is the great cosmic clock in the heavens that will help you keep track of time. Part of retreating involves aligning your-self with what your ancestors knew and understood. Human beings used to be more in touch with the natural cycles of the world, earth cycles, moon cycles, seasonal cycles, solar cycles. Awareness of these cycles is in our DNA – Discover Now Again."

José Humevo clapped his hands in front of my face as he completed the phrase, *Discover Now Again*. The sound surprised me and brought me fully present. He smiled and continued.

"Today is the beginning of a new moon cycle and together we are going to align ourselves with this powerful natural tool. It is not absolutely necessary to be in exact sync with the new moon but it is more effective if you are. Your barefoot walking was not in exact sync with the new moon cycle and yet you were able to derive benefit from that experience.

"In the beginning it is more important to success-fully complete the twenty-eight day cycle than it is to be in exact alignment with the moon. Most people stumble somewhere along the way, and it is better to start again immediately than it is to wait for the next cycle. You knew this intuitively when you slipped on day twenty-four and started over the next day. Because you have experienced it, you understand the consequences of missing a day in the cycle. It is not a lesson that you need to repeat.

"I propose that we begin a new moon cycle togeth-er, each with our own twenty-eight day practice. My prac-tice will be to share the *principles of learning* with you every night for the next twenty-eight nights. Your practice will be to listen to me while we walk together in the dark, no flashlights, no small talk, no distractions. Is there any-thing about this proposal that you do not understand or agree with?

"Do I continue my barefoot walking as well?"

"That is up to you. The beauty of the twenty-eight day practice is the way it blends discipline and freedom, commitment and choice. My theory is this – if I can main-tain a practice for twenty-eight consecutive days, then it is mine. It is in my body. It requires focus, action, and resolve to accomplish such a task. Once the twenty-eight day cycle is complete I am back where I started, free to choose to con-tinue or not. There is no obligation, no guilt, no external compulsion. There is only choice.

"If there is a natural alignment between the practice and myself, then I will continue to incorporate it into my life. If I feel like continuing, I continue. If I don't, I don't. The only way to do this incorrectly is to ignore the natural impulse coming from that place of deep inner knowing.

"Walk barefoot if you want to walk barefoot and don't if you don't. Having said all that, I suggest that you keep your shoes on during our night walking, at least initially. What you do in the daytime is for you to decide. Do you have any other questions?"

"I don't think so."

"Don't think. Feel, intend, act. This is the way forward. It is time to walk."

ALL THAT IS

◆

FOR THE NEXT twenty-eight nights José Humevo and I explored the darkness together. We met on the beach at sunset. Some nights he would begin sharing while we were on the beach, other nights he waited until we were deep in the forest before uttering a single word. I had to learn how to pay equal attention to what he was saying as well as how fast and in what direction he was moving. I ran into his back more than once. His response was always the same – a soft chuckle and the words, "You are not paying attention."

Walking in the dark with José Humevo was an expansive and soothing experience. There was something about the darkness that allowed me to grasp his concepts with relative ease. The sound of his voice penetrated deep into my body, mind, and spirit. One night, early on, he returned to the subject of *All That Is*.

"I would like you to visualize an equilateral triangle, three equal sides and three equal angles. This is my interpretation of the nature of reality. The base of the triangle is *All That Is*, the foundation as well as the contents of the entire universe. There is *no-thing* that is not a part of *All That Is,* or what I refer to as *Ati*."

The word flowed out of his mouth like warm honey, *ah-tea*.

"*Ati* is the ground being of existence. It is God, Allah, Yahweh, the Great Spirit, the Universe. It is called by many names. The name I use is *Ati – All That Is*.

"From a human perspective *Ati* is experienced as the subset of me and *not me*. Me is the aspect of life that I believe I am in control of. *Not me* is everything else. Together they form the left hand and right hand sides of the triangle, respectively. Me and *not me* are supported by *Ati* and are in a symbiotic relationship with one another. If either me or *not me* expand, the other one must contract, and vice versa. Me and *not me* are linked expressions of *All That Is*. They coexist in a dynamic relationship, like the ebb and the flow of the tide.

"Every human being has a unique interpretation of their individual relationship between me and *not me*. Some people treat this relationship as if it were a battle, but I prefer to think of it as a dance. The practice of Advanced Human Awareness is to find that place of balance where me and *not me* support one another. Me and *not me* are equal and opposite aspects of *All That Is*. They are two sides of the same coin.

"All aspects of life are held within the triangle of *Ati*, me, and *not me*. This is the parchment on which I continually sketch the evolving map of my present understanding of Advanced Human Awareness. It is a work in progress that unfolds in the here and now.

"I am a part of *All That Is*. I am spirit and matter, form and energy, substance and inner chi. This is all I have ever been and this is all I will ever be. There is nothing more than this present moment, the eternal now, the point of conscious awareness that moves throughout space and time.

"The only thing that separates me from this direct experience of life is the belief systems I have adopted along the way – the subtle, pervasive, and unquestioned *patterns of being* that are so much a part of my daily experience that they are difficult to see.

"Learning to embrace the relationship between me and *not me* is to experience the dance of yin and yang, ebb and flow, give and take. The secrets of the universe are always available. The trick is to learn how to see beneath the surface layer."

José Humevo's words had a strange effect on me. Instead of struggling to find my way in the dark, I noticed that I was relaxing into the experience. Up until that point I had been trying to keep myself on the trail, focusing with my mind and my eyes. As I relaxed I began to sense the relationship between my body and the trail. I noticed that my body and the trail seemed to be in communication with one another at some deeper level. It was like I was walking the trail and the trail was walking me.

When I shared this sensation with José Humevo he replied that I was experiencing an *aha!* moment of the symbiotic relationship between me and *not me*.

"This is what it feels like to experience the dance of me and *not me*. In this moment you have severed the habitual pattern of being in competition with *not me*. *Not me* is not your enemy, your nemesis, or your antagonist. It is not something that you have to fight, control, or wrestle with. *Not me* is the part of *Ati* that on one hand helps define who we are – it is all that we are not – and on the other hand, it is the part of *Ati* that helps us learn and grow.

"It is all about the way we choose to be in relationship with *not me*. If I choose to view *not me* through the lens of my ego, then it is always a push/pull affair. It becomes a power struggle and I tend to focus on the ways I can protect myself from all that is *not me*. This is a classic example of a faulty behavior pattern that is alive and well in humanity today. I still catch myself falling into this trap from time to time. I understand the symbiotic relationship between me and *not me* as well as anyone I know, but understanding alone is not enough.

"Traveling the path of Advanced Human Awareness is a journey to experience, not a destination to reach. It is a practice that does not end. This practice is an integral part of the human experience. The point of tension between me and *not me* is where evolution unfolds. If I embrace this natural tension, rather than resist it, my view of the world begins to shift.

"The dance between me and *not me* is the way that *Ati* is able to experience itself. Remember, we are spiritual beings. Conscious human awareness is the gift that *Ati* gives to itself, over and over again. Each and every human being has a completely unique understanding of me and *not me*. It is the dance that we all do together that creates the warp and woof of the tapestry that I call *Ati – All That Is*. To experience life in this manner opens the doorway to the path within."

José Humevo stopped talking at that point. He must have sensed that I had reached my limit. My mind was reeling with the concepts he had been sharing. In the darkness of the forest I had a powerful *aha!* moment. I experienced myself as a vehicle through which *Ati* was able to see itself. It was a moment of clarity, and ecstasy, and relief. I watched in amazement as I let go of the burden of attempting to protect myself from *not me*, the struggle of trying to control that which I cannot control, and the futility of trying to always *do it right.*

In that moment my body, my mind, and my spirit all melted into one and I had an experience of cosmic consciousness. I knew that I was part of *Ati* and that *Ati* was part of me. There was no separation, no time, no space. It was like the dream I had had on Orcas Island when José Humevo touched my chest. I was everywhere and nowhere at the same time. It was an instant of pure bliss, and then I was back on the trail.

"Keep walking."

"What?" I attempted to orient myself in the dark.

"Keep walking. Come present to this moment, notice where you are. See the shadows all around you. Hear the wind in the trees. Feel the night air on your face.

Smell the sweetness of the forest. Taste the salt of your tears. Discover Now Again."

It wasn't until José Humevo told me to taste my tears that I realized that I was crying. Tears were streaming down my face. The self imposed expectations I had been carrying around had become so much a part of me that until that moment I did not even realize they were there. As this realization hit me, I felt all the pain and disappointment, the anger and resentment, the jealousy and envy, the rejection and the embarrassment that I had been dragging around for years. I cried out in anguish, my involuntary howl echoing through the night.

"Run!" José Humevo's voice shot through the night like an arrow.

"What?"

"Run. Run. Run for your life!"

Without thinking, I started to run.

"Faster!" His voice faded in the distance.

I ran full speed through the darkness. I have no idea how I found my way. As I ran my howling turned into laughter, but the tears kept flowing. The floodgates had opened and all the pent up emotion I had stored in my body over the years came pouring out of me.

I ran, and I laughed, and I cried until my strength, and my laughter, and my tears were gone. I stopped and stood in the silence, wiping the tears from my face and panting to catch my breath. It seemed like I had been running a very long time and yet I was still somewhere in the forest. Logic told me that I should have reached campus long ago. Where was I?

"You are in the moment."

José Humevo was standing next to me. I was too exhausted to be startled.

"The darkness and your intention to learn opened a crack in space and time and you slipped quite naturally into the here and now. This is what it feels like to Discover Now Again. This is another way to be. The way you have been is only one of an infinite number of possible choices available to you.

"Awareness is what we experience, it is not who we are. Your me is much more pliable than you have imagined, and so is your *not me*. Up until this moment you have been living your life based on a description of reality that has been passed down from generation to generation. There is nothing wrong with this other than the fact that it severely limits your choices.

"Like most human beings you are a paradox. Your intake portal is quite open, and yet it is rigid in its relatively open state. There is more fluidity available to you. Tonight you tasted the possibilities of what a greater level of fluidity feels like. We live in a world overflowing with magic, awe, and mystery that you have merely caught a glimpse of. The path within will lead the way, to the degree that you are willing.

"We have talked a great deal about awareness and tonight you tapped into intention. Awareness and intention are two of the four components of the *learning cycle*. This is another valuable tool that I will share with you, but not tonight. Tonight we must find our way back to the world, as you know it. It takes energy to remain consciously in the moment. Now it is time for you to rest. Close your eyes and follow my voice."

In less than a minute I felt pavement under my feet. We were behind the library. In the dim glow from the path lights I watched as José Humevo scanned my body. He seemed satisfied with whatever it was he was seeing. He put his hand on the top of my head and gently squeezed it three times. Then he spoke.

"Go directly home and get some rest. I will see you again tomorrow."

MAGIC OF THE FEET

◆

José Humevo was relatively quiet for the next few evenings. I sensed that he was allowing me time to gather my energy. The night of running through the forest had exhausted me at a very deep level. When I asked him about it he repeated what he had said to me earlier. "It takes energy to remain consciously in the moment."

José Humevo was an enigma. At times he would talk non-stop, explaining his principles and practices with amazing clarity. Other times I found him completely obtuse or so reluctant to speak that he appeared almost mute. Did he do this to keep me on my toes or was he like this with everyone? The answer to this question seemed to vacillate back and forth as our night walking continued. On the fifteenth night we switched roles. José Humevo informed me that it was time for me to lead. We were sitting on the beach, enjoying the sunset when he began to speak.

"Walking a path at night is not the same as walking that path in the daylight with your eyes closed. You have walked these trails many times. Do not allow this fact to give you false confidence or assurance. In the darkness the earth beneath your feet becomes more expansive. It opens a doorway to a level of perception that is not accessible during the day. This is why you were able to run for so long the other night and still not leave the forest. You were not on the trails of the day.

"The same thing is true for barefoot walking, but the shift is less dramatic. Where night walking is expansive, barefoot walking is grounding. Night walking connects us to the cosmos. Barefoot walking connects us to the earth. They each open a doorway to perception that is not normally available. On one hand they are similar and on the other hand they are completely unique.

"There is a third way to open this door. It is a practice you can do during the day or during the night, with shoes or without them. It can be done with relative subtlety or exaggerated flair. It is a flexible, pragmatic, and useful addition to your bag of tools. I call this practice the Altered Perception Experience walk – the *ape walk*. It is a primate-like gait that creates an Altered Perception Experience, not unlike night walking or barefoot walking. It looks like this."

José Humevo stood up and turned sideways so that I could see his profile. He lowered his hips a few inches by bending his knees, tipped his pelvis forward, and started walking. His arms swung loosely at his sides as he moved back and forth along the beach in front of me. His hips remained in that lowered position the entire time, which shifted his weight onto the balls of his feet. His movements were indeed somewhat ape-like and at the same time he looked remarkably graceful.

After making a few passes up and down the beach José Humevo stopped in front of me. He raised his hands to his armpits, tilted his head side to side several times, and made a comical ape-like sound deep in his throat. He laughed as he motioned for me to join him.

I stood up, looked around to make sure no one was watching, and did my best to mimic his movements. It was awkward at first, but within a few minutes I was able to follow him with relative ease. The thing I noticed most was that my feet felt much more stable on the ground. The more I walked, the better it felt. There was an odd familiarity about the movement.

We practiced on the beach and José Humevo helped me fine-tune my technique. "Focus on the area between the base of your big toe and the rest of your toes, push forward with your weight equally divided on either side of this spot. It is a moving meditation. If you find that your attention has drifted away simply bring it back to this area again and again.

"Adjust your upper body to match the terrain. Lean forward when going up hill and lean back when going down. For night walking slow the entire process down and exaggerate the way you lift your feet to avoid tripping over unseen objects near the ground. Let's go for a test ride, you lead." Then he started to sing, "I will follow you..."

The sound of his singing turned into laughter and then faded into silence as we entered the darkness. A full moon was rising but was too low in the sky to provide any useful light. I had become accustomed to following José Humevo on the trails. Now it was time for me to lead and I struggled to find my way. José Humevo allowed me flounder for ten minutes before he finally spoke.

"Try closing your eyes. The limited visual information you are receiving is doing you more harm than good. This is an Altered Perception Experience. Use something else to find your way."

"Like what?"

"Your feet, your intention, your intuition. Find that place inside that helped you run through the darkness the other night. That place is not inside your head. Turn off your mind and turn on your intuition. Be clear about your intention. Practice the *ape walk* and allow your feet to show you the way."

It didn't make sense to close my eyes while walking in the forest at night. My mind insisted that I needed to use what little light there was to help me orient myself. However, José Humevo had a point. I had not relied on my eyes the night that I ran through the darkness. I closed my eyes and proceeded with caution. As my pace decreased, so did my breathing. I could feel my feet making solid contact with the ground.

"Let your body guide you. Trust your gut instincts. If your belly turns to the left or the right, trust that movement and follow it. Relax your mind, relax your body, and allow your feet to lead the way. This is an Altered

Perception Experience. This is another way to be."

The words of José Humevo guided me until I was able to guide myself. The more I relaxed into the experience the easier it became. I focused on the *ape walk* and my body led me through the darkness.

"Now open your eyes and enjoy the experience without engaging habitual mental patterns. The stimulation to your eyes is no different than the stimulation of the night air on your face. There is nothing you have to do with this stimulation other than to notice it. There is no need to control it, or define it, or explain it. Allow it to be there, nothing else is required."

We walked in silence for a few more minutes before the lights of the library came into view. The sight of the building triggered a familiar mental pattern and I watched myself shift from altered perception to a more normal state of being. The shift was subtle but surprisingly jarring to my body. I turned my back to the light.

"The transition between these two worlds will get easier as you increase your flexibility. Be patient and allow this process to unfold over time."

José Humevo moved his hands to his armpits once again, screamed like a monkey, and chased me all the way to the library. I stopped when I hit the pavement but he kept on running. He turned his head as he passed me. "You did well tonight!"

I laughed all the way to the parking lot and felt extremely alert as I drove home. Tammy was in a talkative mood and I was surprised by how present I was to the conversation. My ability to focus so clearly on what she was saying seemed to pull her deeper and deeper into her story. We talked late into the night. The interaction moved our relationship to a new level of honesty and trust.

The following morning I noticed an increased awareness of how I was moving as I crossed Red Square on my way to class. I took a short barefoot hike after lunch and adopted a modified version of the *ape walk* as I moved. My feet were able to adjust or react to the surface of the trail in a manner that was precise and slightly awkward at the same time. When I met José Humevo at the beach that evening I shared my experience with him.

"You are discovering the magic of the feet."

"The magic of the feet?"

He started to speak, paused, looked at me with a curious expression and then paused again. "I wasn't planning on having this discussion so soon, but now that you have brought it up I am going to trust that the timing is right.

"The feet and the hands of human beings are expressions of yin and yang, respectively, and over the years the two have fallen out of balance with one another. As a species we have become mesmerized by the cleverness of our hands. The opposable thumb of Homo sapiens is indeed a marvel of physical evolution and should be recognized as such. However, myopic focus of any kind tends to have serious limitations over the long haul.

"Our puffed-up attitude about the greatness of humanity keeps us from acknowledging the places where we have lost our way. In our enthusiastic embrace of all things human we have lost sight of the inner wisdom and the balance of those from which we sprang. One thing that all other primates instinctively know how to do is to live in harmony and balance with the environment that supports them. Humanity has lost track of this knowledge. This is a rather serious oversight.

"It is our lack of direct contact with the earth that has allowed us to wander so far off the path of sensitivity to our environment. We cannot continue to gobble up our natural resources and scatter garbage across the landscape indefinitely. This unchecked behavior is a glaring example of a *pattern of being* that makes absolutely no sense, and yet it seems to be accepted without question.

"The direction that humanity is currently heading in is a dead end street. It is time for us to return to a path of sustainability. We have created a series of problems that are so complex and intertwined that it has paralyzed our ability to solve them. The solution to this problem does not lie in creating greater and greater levels of complexity. The solution is found in simplicity. The solution is, and always has been, at our feet.

"I believe that the way out of this situation is through re-activating the connection with our feet. The relationship between the human hand and the human brain has had a major role in our evolutionary development. This relationship has created the high water marks of human culture – art, music, mathematics, and the written word. The problem is that there has not been a corresponding development between the feet and the brain.

"We wrap our feet in protective gear and cut them off from direct contact with the earth. We are the only animals on the planet that experiences this level of disconnection from the environment in which we live. It is the loss of direct contact with the being that supports and sustains us that has allowed us to stray so far off the path of sustainability and common sense.

"Our feet are our connection to the earth, and that connection is the counter balance to the complexity of the hand/brain relationship. The absence of an equal and opposite development of the foot/brain relationship in human beings has created atrophy in the portion of the brain that understands the importance and the necessity of sustainability. This imbalance is what has allowed us to carelessly pollute our rivers, decimate our forests, pave over our farmland, and create weapons of annihilation. These are not rational acts for a species interested in longevity.

"The water in the pot we are in keeps getting hotter and hotter and no one seems to care. We have allowed our world to become too complex, too masculine, too linear, too yang. In order to come into balance it is time to fully acknowledge and embrace our feminine, our intuitive, and our yin aspects.

"This is the way forward. The answer is at our feet. The answer is in the connection between our feet and the environment that supports and sustains us. This is why I chose barefoot walking as your initiation practice. I wanted to see if you had the patience, persistence, and perseverance to complete a twenty-eight day cycle, and I wanted to see how you would respond to re-awakening the connection with your feet. It was the recounting of your experience that you shared at the Art Deco that convinced Jackson and me that you were ready to take the next step.

"A journey of a thousand miles begins with the first step, the answer is at your feet, the pathway will unfold before you – these are the clues hidden in our language. Our hands connect us to the wonders of complexity. Our feet connect us to the joys of simplicity. Complexity and simplicity are one another's *not me*. They are two sides of the same coin. Neither one is at its best without the other."

José Humevo stood up and gestured for me to join him. "Do not over-process any of this. The best thing you can do now is to come fully present to the moment. Lead us through the darkness and let us discover what other secrets the Altered Perception Experience walk might reveal. Allow the earth to ground your body. Allow the darkness to expand your mind. Allow my words to settle deep into your spirit. You will naturally hold onto that which resonates with your core and release that which does not. Your only task at this time is to Discover Now Again."

WHEN THE STUDENT IS READY

◆

FOR THE NEXT two weeks I led José Humevo and myself through the darkness of the forest. We walked, he talked, and together we began to deepen the foundation of our relationship. Clearly, he was the guide and I was the one being guided, but it was not a traditional student/teacher arrangement. José Humevo did not use the word teacher. He insisted that he had nothing to teach. He told me repeatedly that his intent was to help himself and others unlearn the *patterns of being* that limit human potential. He consistently referred to himself as a learning guide and an evolutionary.

As far as I could tell José Humevo practiced the *principles of learning* in his daily life. He consistently confronted his fears, demonstrated humor and humility in everything he did, and embraced mistakes whenever he

119

encountered them. He did not try to impress me with his knowledge. He gave me simple, honest, and direct feedback on my actions and my attitudes. As our relationship developed my respect and trust grew, allowing me to be increasingly authentic with him. José Humevo referred to this as learning the art of *into-me-see*.

"Intimacy is nothing more than the willingness to be seen by another. It is the fear of not being good enough that keeps human beings from fully exposing themselves to one another. Fear is the problem. Trust is the solution. Courage is the way. This is the fourth *principle of learning*.

"The one thing that I most want to help you unlearn is the belief that you are less than perfect just the way you are. It is this subtle yet pervasive *pattern of being* that keeps us separate from one another. What would life look like, feel like, be like if we didn't waste time and energy hiding, protecting, or defending ourselves from the perceived inspections, judgments, and onslaughts of others?

"There is nothing embarrassing, incorrect, or flawed about the essence of who or what you are. You are a unique expression of *All That Is* with no more or less value than any other expression of *All That Is*. Any pecking order or value system that you may have adopted is based on flawed human beliefs, opinions, and assumptions that have mutated over time. None of this has anything to do with the essence of *Ati*.

"Our task is not to attempt to force or control life. Our task is to relax and to practice coming into alignment with self. Coming into alignment with self allows us to fully appreciate and embrace the wonder and the joy of this mysterious experience that I call Advanced Human Awareness. It is a truly remarkable experience that most people miss because they are so preoccupied with *doing it right.*

"We become so caught up in the details that we miss the larger experience. Advanced Human Awareness is a magical and mysterious thing. It is life experiencing life. It is *All That Is* experiencing itself through an infinite number of individual and unique perspectives all at the same time. This is the soup we are in. This is our natural state of being.

"There is nothing we need to do in order to be in this state; we are always already there. There are, however some things we need to undo, to unlearn, to release, to let go of, in order to recognize and engage with this natural state of being. The first things to let go of are tension and fear. When tension is gone, we relax. When fear is gone, we trust. What could be easier than to relax and to trust? And yet, for most of us it is the hardest thing in the world. Why is this?"

He paused, arched his eyebrows, and then answered his own question. "It is because we have been taught to control and direct our lives in ways that do not serve us. We struggle and fight with *not me*. Sometimes we win, sometimes we lose, either way the struggle continues. The effort required to get ahead or to stay ahead eventually wears us down. We get tired, we get old, and finally we die. And in that moment of death every conscious human being recognizes the futility of the struggle. We do not need to wait until death is staring us in the face in order to experience alignment with self.

"There is a time and a place outside the boundaries of the physical world where we are able to observe and understand the human experience, where we are able to laugh at our foolish habits and beliefs. From that place of clarity we are able to see the folly of our ways. We tell ourselves that we will do better next time. Then we go back into the game and forget all that we ever knew. We accept the current description of the world without question and join the struggle to control all that is *not me*. We fall back into the same old trap over and over again. We become blinded by the minutia and forget about the larger, slower, foundational patterns of human existence.

"It does not have to be this way. There is another way to be. That way is to relax, to trust, to remember how to come into alignment with who we really are. It is the *aha!* moment that we have talked about. This moment is a doorway, a pivot point on which to turn our understanding of life in a new direction. We are spiritual beings having a human experience. This is a profoundly different lens through which to view reality. It is an opportunity to recognize and embrace a new understanding of the foundational patterns of Advanced Human Awareness.

"Many people attach significance to the specific details of an *aha!* experience. This focus on detail tends to reinforce old belief systems or will occasionally create an entirely new belief system. This is how religious, political, social, and psychological patterns are started and sustained in any given culture at any given time.

"There is nothing inherently wrong with these patterns. They are unique expressions of individuality and deserve to be celebrated. They are the high notes that provide the melodic richness of the human experience. However, they are not the be all and end all. The slower rhythms should be honored and embraced as well. They provide the stability and depth of the human experience. They are the beat of the dance of life.

"Both the richness and the depth are needed. They are bound together in a symbiotic relationship. One cannot fully express without the other. The problem occurs whenever we believe that one pattern is more worthy of existence than another. When we take ourselves too seriously, when we believe our beliefs to be absolute, when we mistake the description of life for life itself – this is when we get into trouble.

"There is nothing we need to force or manipulate. There is only an experience to experience, and that experience can be experienced any way we choose. The secret is not to use our life force to attempt to control all that is *not me*. This is a foolish investment of time and energy. In the long run it will not yield a positive return.

"A wiser investment is to learn how to recognize and appreciate the infinite and eternal abundance of *All That Is*. This adds richness and depth to the human experience, individually and collectively, and this adds richness and depth to *All That Is*. This is the seed of the evolutionary impulse.

"Life is a practice, not a performance, and it should be treated as such. I will never do it perfectly and I will never get it done. There is no ultimate finish line. There is no one to impress or to receive approval from. There is only me and *not me* and we are doing a dance. It is called the dance of life.

"The world around me is doing what it is doing and being how it is being. That is its job. My job is to choose, consciously or unconsciously, to Embrace, Allow, or Resist whatever is unfolding around me. This is where free will comes into play. I refer to this as the *ear practice* – Embrace, Allow, Resist. It is a way of listening, not only with my ears, but also with my body, my mind, and my spirit. The *ear practice* is a tool that increases my awareness of how I am choosing to interact with *not me*.

"To Embrace is to engage positively with what is. To Allow is to accept neutrally what is. To Resist is to react negatively to what is. There is an appropriate time and place for each one of these responses. The important thing is to be conscious about the choice. Am I consciously choosing my response, or am I unconsciously reacting to the situation I find myself in, right here and right now? This is the question I must ask myself moment to moment. The choice to respond or to react is offered up again and again, for the duration of my life.

"Am I fully present to this moment that is unfolding in front of the individual point of conscious awareness that I call me? The answer to this question determines the experience of my life. Is life out to get me, or is life trying to *get me out*? Does it want to fight or does it want to dance? What is my relationship to my life? Am I a victim of, or am I a co-creator with, the life that I live?

"Blaming *not me* for all the things that are wrong in

124

my life will not move me forward. I am stuck where I am stuck until I choose to be free. The problem as well as the solution always lies within. The world around me is a direct reflection of my own internal projections. The most effective way to change my experience of the world is to change myself. This can be a stepping stone or a stumbling block; the choice is up to me. *All That Is* will show me the way if and when I have eyes to see."

José Humevo stopped talking and we finished our walk in silence. He had a pattern of filling me to the point of overload and then creating the time and space for the information to sink in. The expansiveness of the darkness seemed to facilitate this process. Every night for the next two weeks he would introduce a new principle or practice, or return to and expand upon a topic that we had already discussed. Whenever I started to feel overwhelmed by the sheer volume of his information he would remind me to simply allow the words to wash over me, to relax and to trust that I would absorb whatever I was ready to take in.

By the twenty-eighth night I was feeling confident about my ability to lead us safely through the woods. I had learned how to listen to José Humevo and focus on where I was going at the same time. At some point I had settled into the place where his words seeped into my awareness as the trail unfolded beneath my feet. When I finally got out of the way, it all flowed quite effortlessly. On that final night he offered up two more learning principles.

"Remember to consciously work with your portals. Allow the information to flow in and allow it to flow out. There is nothing that you have to hold on to. That which is

in alignment with you will find its way into your awareness. That which is not in alignment will simply pass
through you. This is not something that you need to force.
When the student is ready the teaching appears. This is the
fifth *principle of learning*.

"I spent many years wandering the far corners of
the earth searching for my teacher. I was looking for the
teacher in the form of a human being and kept missing the
teaching that was always available to me. It took me a long
time to understand that the teaching is the teacher. The
teaching is always with me and is accessible as soon as I
am able to recognize it as such.

"This is why I do not use the term teacher to
describe myself. I do not want you to confuse the teacher
with the teaching, for they are not the same. I am passing
information to you but I am not the way. The way is inside
of you. It always has been and it always will be. My intention is to help you rediscover the path within. My job is to
prime the pump, to get the water flowing. I am neither
pump nor water. That is between you and *Ati*. I am here to
lubricate the system, that is all.

"Tonight concludes our twenty-eight day cycle and
tomorrow it will be time to rest and take an in-breath. It has
been a valuable experience for me to have shared with you
during this period. It has helped me clarify my thoughts. I
have other matters to which I must attend. During the next
moon cycle I encourage you to continue your night walking, this time on your own. You will discover that walking
alone in the dark is different from walking with another
human being. The trail alone at night moves to the next

level of reality.

"If I have not returned before the end of your solo night hiking practice, take a short break and begin a new cycle. You will know what to do when the time comes. Remember to be consistent with your practice during the twenty-eight days and to release all obligations once you have completed the cycle. It is of utmost importance not to succumb to guilt, fear, or habit once the cycle is complete. The *not doing* is as important as the doing. Is there anything about these instructions that you do not understand?"

"Why are you leaving now?"

"This is not a question of understanding. It is a statement of your desire to remain within your comfort zone. I am leaving. How you choose to respond to this is up to you. If you Embrace it, it creates one experience. If you Allow it, it creates a different experience. If you Resist it, it creates a third experience. Use the *ear practice* to expand your awareness. Are you Embracing, Allowing, or Resisting my decision to leave? My actions do not dictate your experience.

"We have spent the last twenty-eight nights together and now I am leaving. Is the glass half empty or is the glass half full? The answer to that question is for you to decide. No one else gets to make that decision for you, unless you foolishly give that power away. This is the way it works. If you want to experience Advanced Human Awareness you cannot continue to wallow in your old unconscious *patterns of being*. I have told you before that this path is not easy. If you want to evolve you have to do the work required. You cannot stay where you are and move forward at the same time. This is the sixth *principle of learning*.

"You have to be willing to step outside of your comfort zone if you want to continue to learn and grow. It requires focus, action, and resolve to unlock the secrets hidden inside your DNA. Discover Now Again, open to the here and now, and stretch Advanced Human Awareness as far as you can.

"Each and every one of us is a unique expression of *All That Is*. We are all bozos on this bus and we are all brilliant points of light shining in the darkness. The world around you is filled to the brim with magic, awe, and mystery. There is no limit to what you can do. Open your portals, be willing to change, embrace human evolution, and go as far as you can go. This is the gift that you give to yourself. This is the gift of *Ati*."

There was something odd about the way he completed his last statement. There was an unusual finality to his voice. I was aware of this on one level but mostly I was focused on listening to his words and finding my way in the dark. In the silence that followed I noticed that I could not hear José Humevo behind me. It wasn't so much that I couldn't hear his footsteps – José Humevo made very little noise when he walked. It was more that I could not feel his presence.

I stopped in my tracks and turned around, and in that instant I knew that he was gone. The hair on the back of my head stood on end. I called out his name, more out of habit and nervousness than anything else.

There was no reply. A rush of fear swept through me. The deep loneliness that had been circling around me for years burst through my defenses. I prepared for the impact but the dreaded event did not materialize. My fear of finding myself all alone was a phantom, a Fantasized Experience Appearing Real.

While my mind was attempting to sort this out, my body started doing the *ape walk*. The faster I moved the more my mind relaxed. The hair on the back of my head was still on end but I realized that it was not so much from fear as it was from excitement. As my mind relaxed I was able to grasp that José Humevo came and went the way he did quite deliberately. It was an exercise to stretch my boundaries and keep me limber.

"Transition points are where flexibility is tested and revealed. This is the seventh *principle of learning*."

It took me a moment to realize that it was my inner voice and not the words of José Humevo that I was hearing. I laughed out loud as I glided through the darkness. José Humevo was a master. He had skillfully led me to the seventh *principle of learning*. Energy was flowing through my body, and in that instant I understood that fear and excitement were different interpretations of the same physical sensation. One was constrictive, the other was expansive.

There was a depth to this awareness that hinted that this knowledge had always been with me, just out of reach, veiled behind my unquestioned habits, assumptions, and beliefs. It wasn't so much a new understanding as it was an alignment with something that had always been present.

The lights from campus came into view and pulled me out of the darkness. I found myself split between a sense of relief and a sense of disappointment. As I listened to the internal debate going on within me I noticed a softer, calmer voice as well. It was the voice of José Humevo echoing in my head.

"When the student is ready the teaching appears."

INTO THE DARKNESS

———◆———

As much as I told myself that the strange comings and goings of José Humevo were understandable, it did nothing to prevent the corresponding rattling that I felt in my day to day life. I returned to the beach the following evening at sunset and felt a sense of loss as I gazed into the western sky without José Humevo by my side. The new moon was not ready to show itself and I hiked back to campus in the twilight before darkness fell.

I heard marimba music as I emerged from the trail and approached the library. I entered the large vaulted room that functioned as foyer, gathering spot, and performance space and found the *Geoduck Marimba Ensemble* jamming away. A hundred sweaty bodies were dancing to the infectious beat. I joined in and let myself move with total abandon.

Dancing that night was a welcome counter point to my night hiking. I had not been aware of how much my training with José Humevo had put a damper on my social life. I saw many old friends and met a few new ones. I danced, I sweated, I laughed with delight. I caught myself feeling almost guilty for having so much fun before a little voice inside my head reminded me that *not doing* is as important as doing. Old habits are hard to break, especially for those of us with Nordic blood running through our veins. By midnight I was having no regrets. By 2:00 am I was in bed with Bonnie Keough.

Bonnie was a theater major. We had gotten to know one another a couple of years earlier when we were in an interdisciplinary program together. I had been somewhat smitten by her playful personality, her expressive gestures, her long auburn hair. We had worked on a project together but had not established a relationship outside of that context.

She had fallen off my radar screen before we had a chance to connect in any meaningful way. She was not on campus the summer that I stayed to work in the library and then I left for my Orcas Island adventure. I had not seen her again until we bumped into one another on the dance floor. We exchanged a hug and stayed in close proximity. As the evening unfolded we found ourselves moving closer and closer to one another, first through movement, then through conversation, and finally through touch. When the music came to an end we moved to a gathering at her house. When the gathering ended we found ourselves in bed together. It all flowed together quite naturally and at the same time we were both a little surprised to find ourselves in this situation.

Bonnie had just finished directing a one-act play and I felt like I had just completed boot camp with José Humevo. Both of us were ready for a break from the intensity and action of the past couple of months. We eased effortlessly into sexual exploration although we did not fully consummate the relationship. We shared what we knew about the art of sensual pleasure and practiced our newly acquired skills for the next several hours. There was a slightly awkward sound to my voice when I looked at Bonnie in the morning and asked, "Now what?"

She responded by tickling me mercilessly. This turned into a full-blown wrestling match that ended with some sweet kisses. My stomach started to growl. When I suggested a trip to the Art Deco, Bonnie's eyes lit up. Appreciation for comfort food was one thing we had in common. We headed into downtown Olympia and traded stories over breakfast.

Bonnie was from the East Coast and I was a native Washingtonian. She grew up with money, I was middle class. She was a recovering Catholic, I was a non-practicing Lutheran. Bonnie seemed to know exactly where she was going, I felt like I was still finding my way. We were so different that it was challenging to connect and yet there was this undeniable connection between us. It was an odd combination of feeling like strangers, sweethearts, and friends. By the time we had finished eating we were both shaking our heads. What we did have in common was a good sense of humor, a willingness to be honest with one another, and a strong physical attraction. With this as a foundation we agreed to move forward one step at a time.

The one area where I felt conflicted was around my relationship with José Humevo. I had agreed to keep the details of our relationship private and I wasn't sure how this was going to mesh with establishing an open and honest relationship with Bonnie. I decided to put the question on hold.

When evening rolled around I headed to the beach and found a new moon in the western sky. The visual image captured my attention. I watched until the last light from the tip of the amber crescent moon disappeared below the horizon. I stood up. It was time to begin my next twenty-eight day cycle and this time I would be flying solo. I turned and headed into the woods.

As I stepped into the darkness I had José Humevo and Bonnie Keough very much on my mind. Their presence inside my head made me feel that much more alone in the forest. The camaraderie and connection that I had experienced while walking and listening to José Humevo had been replaced by a sense of fear and isolation. I told myself to release the fear, but I couldn't seem to shake it. The more I pushed it away, the more it pushed back at me. I could feel the darkness closing in around me.

This feeling increased until I stopped and began to consciously focus on slowing down my breathing. As my breathing relaxed, so did the muscles in my shoulders and jaw. My belly softened and my mind began to clear. Standing in the darkness, focusing on slowing and deepening my breath, I recalled a conversation that I had had with

José Humevo during one of our night walks.

"I am an attractor to the world around me. What I focus on is what I draw to myself. The dance of me and *not me* does not recognize positive or negative, it only recognizes intensity and focus. The greater the intensity, the greater the focus, the greater the attraction. Preciseness of thought and language become increasingly important as I travel further down the path of Advanced Human Awareness."

José Humevo paused and gave me a look that told me to pay attention. "If I tell a child not to spill the glass of milk that is sitting precariously close to the edge of the table, what is likely to happen?"

"The child spills the milk?"

"Quite likely. How does this change if I turn up the volume and yell, 'don't spill the milk' in a frantic manner?"

"It increases the chances of the milk being spilled?"

"*Aha*! The greater the intensity, the greater the focus, the greater the attraction. There is a part of the child that hears the urgency but not the qualifier. What comes through is, 'spill the milk'. The next thing you know, milk is on the floor.

"There is a part of the human brain that is just like that child. It hears the intensity and focus of the communication but not the qualifiers, do or don't. What would be a more effective way to speak to this child?"

"What do you mean?"

"Let me ask it another way. What are you attempting to communicate?"

"Not to spill the milk."

"You are not paying attention. What is your intent?"

I attempted to hide the irritation in my voice. "My intent is to prevent the child from spilling the glass of milk."

José Humevo laughed. "You are getting warmer. How would you most effectively communicate that intent? What would you say?"

"Honey, be careful with that glass of milk."

José Humevo laughed again. "Your attitude is less than charming, but your awareness has improved. Tell the child what you want, not what you don't want. The same is true for the child inside of you. Tell it what to do, not what not to do. Keep your communication clear and concise and focus on the outcome you desire. This subtle shift creates a dramatic change in awareness, understanding, and knowledge of *not me*."

I don't remember what we were talking about when José Humevo used this example of the child and the milk but I knew that the principle applied to my current situation. I had been focused on getting rid of my fear instead of relaxing my body. The more I pushed the fear away, the more it pushed back at me. The fear decreased as I slowed down my breathing. Within thirty seconds my experience had completely turned around. Instead of resisting the darkness, I began to embrace it.

Every time I walked in the dark it was a different experience. Some nights it was easy and enjoyable, some nights it felt like work, and some nights I would find my inner demons, those aspects of myself that kept me small.

By the end of the first week I realized that fear of the dark was really fear of knowing myself. The darkness was not an evil force out to get me. It was an aspect of *not me* that was trying to *get me out*. One night it became clear to me that I was no more vulnerable walking alone at night than I was walking down the street in broad daylight with a friend.

When I distilled it down, I saw that night walking by myself and day walking with a friend were each an experience of me surrounded by *not me*. One experience was relatively new, which made it exciting or scary, depending on my point of view, and the other experience was familiar, which made it ordinary and comfortable. The impact of this awareness was twofold. One, I began to be more relaxed in the darkness and two, I began to be more alert during the day.

In some ways I was more surprised by the pattern of my daytime habits than I was about my ability to relax into the darkness. I was beginning to understand what José Humevo meant when he talked about *patterns of being*. Throughout the day I would catch myself engaged in unconscious acts of Embracing, Allowing, or Resisting whatever I was interacting with – an irritating person, rush hour traffic, frolicking in the woods with Bonnie.

I had a knee-jerk reaction to each one of these. I also had a choice. I did not have to remain locked into my habitual responses. The decision to consciously Embrace, Allow, or Resist any event or experience in my life was always in front of me. I had heard these words before, in books, and films, and songs but I didn't really get it until that very moment. The concept moved out of my head and into my body, and with that shift, everything changed.

I found myself engaging the *ear practice* more and more. I would slip in and out of this state of awareness throughout the day. It would come and go like the wind or the tide. Sometimes I was Mr. Enlightenment and sometimes I was totally unconscious, caught up in some old tape loop, replaying it for the hundredth time inside my head. At first I judged myself for not doing it perfectly – an old Scandinavian *pattern of being* – but over time I began to loosen my expectations. José Humevo was right, it took energy to remain present to the moment and I did not yet have enough to stay there all the time. I had to keep reminding myself that making mistakes along the way was an integral part of the learning process.

OWL MEDICINE

◆────────────

MY NOCTURNAL DISAPPEARANCES eventually became a source of curiosity for Bonnie. The issue I had put on hold a few weeks earlier had finally come home to roost. If I wanted to move forward with her, I was going to have to find a way to explain myself. The times that I completed my night hikes before I went to see her worked out fine. It was when we hooked up before I had walked that proved to be challenging.

One evening near the end of my twenty-eight day cycle Bonnie hosted a potluck dinner at her house. Dinner was followed by dancing, which was followed by conversation and laughter into the wee hours of the morning. After the gathering broke up, I crawled into bed with Bonnie and drifted off to sleep. I woke up a few hours later with that same sinking feeling I had felt on Christmas morning when I realized that I had forgotten to barefoot walk the day before. I looked at my watch; it was 3:00 am, still dark outside.

I started to move but Bonnie and I were tangled up like a couple of puppies during naptime. I pulled my arm out from under her body and she immediately rolled back onto it. As I attempted to free it again she started talking in her sleep. I had to perform an amazing series of gymnastic moves at tai chi speed in order to extract myself from the human knot we had created.

It took me a good five minutes to successfully complete my task without waking her up. It took a few more minutes to locate my clothes in the dark, and another thirty seconds or so to open, slip through, and close her remarkably squeaky bedroom door. Once I made it to the living room I was home free, or so I thought.

I could not find my shoes in the jumbled mess inside the front door. There was someone sleeping on the couch and I didn't want to wake them up by turning on the light. I decided that it was time to combine barefoot walking with night hiking. I slipped my down vest over my tee shirt and stepped outside. The air was crisp and clear and I could see stars through the broken cloud cover. The dew on the grass stimulated my feet and helped to wake me up.

Bonnie lived near Evergreen. There was a path between her house and campus that hooked up with the trails that I normally walked. I crossed the field behind her house and headed for that path. About ten feet from the edge of the forest I noticed a movement out of the corner of my eye and turned to see a Great Horned Owl diving directly at my head. I raised my forearm and let out an involuntary scream. Everything shifted into slow motion.

The owl swerved to his right, his wings thrusting forward three times as he attempted to change speed and direction. The air currents created by this motion washed over my face. I tried to bend down and step back at the same time and tripped over a large rock behind me. My arms flailed upward in an attempt to regain my balance. As I started to fall I had a strange sense of overlapping perspectives. I watched the event unfold in slow motion from my normal, first person, point of view and at the same time I was able to see it from a third person perspective, as if I were standing ten or fifteen feet away from the scene.

I watched as the man's forearm and the bird's talons collided with one another. I could see that the man hit the bird as much as the bird flew into the man. The owl tumbled sideways and nearly hit the ground. It swooped upward in an arcing motion and landed on a low branch of a nearby tree.

Simultaneously, the man was knocked off balance. He arched backwards as his feet came off the ground. He sailed a short distance through the air before landing flat on his back. On the moment of impact I returned exclusively to my first person point of view. My sense of time returned to normal as well.

The impact knocked the wind out of me and it took me a few seconds to catch my breath. I could see the silhouette of the owl on the branch. I reached around for a rock to throw and jumped to my feet in anger. I felt like I had been attacked and wanted to retaliate. However, as I stood there glaring at the owl, feeling very much like a victim, the third person perspective kept playing itself over and over in my mind. The longer I thought about it the more I realized that I had hit the owl as much as it had hit me. In some odd manner we had crossed one another's path. It was awkward, but it had not been malicious or seriously injurious to either one of us. I had a sense that the owl had mistaken my bushy blonde hair for a rabbit or a cat. The look in his eyes when we were face to face revealed as much surprise as mine must have.

My angry stare softened and I dropped the rock that I had been clenching in my fist. We held eye contact for a few seconds, the owl blinked his huge eyes three times, and disappeared into the forest. As the darkness swallowed his image I felt blood dripping down my arm. I determined that the short duration of my night hike had been offset by the intensity of the experience. I turned and headed back to the house.

I walked into the bathroom, closed the door and flipped on the light. I checked my arm and found three parallel scratches about an inch apart and three inches long. The cuts were not deep but they were bloody and ragged. I flushed the wound with hydrogen peroxide and wrapped it with some gauze that I found in the medicine cabinet.

I crawled into bed and snuggled close to Bonnie. I had started shaking when I was in the bathroom and hoped that her body heat would warm me up. I think I was in mild shock. The adult inside of me was mystified by what had just happened with the owl. The little boy inside of me was frightened. I focused on the curiosity and did my best to ignore the fear, but it would not go away. My body continued to shake. I pulled myself even closer to Bonnie and allowed the child within to express its fear. My body shook two or three times and then relaxed. As soon as I allowed the feelings that I had considered inappropriate and embarrassing to be expressed, they disappeared. I had been resisting those feelings. As José Humevo had told me on more than one occasion, "What we resist, persists."

The little boy in me simply wanted to be acknowledged. Ignoring the part of me that I considered weak or fragile was a *pattern of being* in the culture that I grew up in that did not produce the desired results. I had been putting on the facade of being a secure young man, acting like I was in control and sure of myself. The truth is that the child within never really goes away. It needs an occasional gentle touch, loving hug, or reassuring word. It is only when I ignore that child that it begins to act out in inappropriate ways, causing me to ignore, and suppress, and hide even more. It is a vicious circle that is broken by Embracing and Allowing. Not by Resisting. My entire being relaxed as soon as I had this awareness. In the stillness of the night I heard an owl hoot three times in the distance. I fell asleep and eased into dreaming.

I was riding on the back of an owl, my legs straddling her body, my arms around her neck. The wind blowing against my face was forceful and cold. I pulled myself closer into the downy softness and warmth of her feathers.

I could feel the muscles in her back flexing beneath

me as she adjusted her wings to the shifting air currents. We were gliding over a snow-covered mountain. The leading edge of a jagged glacier was breaking off in enormous chunks. Crystal clear water melting from the ice began to trickle down the mountainside. The trickle became a stream and the stream became a river, churning with white water as it pushed against the boulders in its path.

The owl swooped down close to the river. The roar of the rushing water filled my ears. There was spray on my face. The owl dropped even closer, inches above the water and the roar grew loader. It was like standing next to a speeding freight train. My excitement started slipping towards fear and I held on with all my strength. My entire body was vibrating and I began to lose my grip. The fear intensified, my muscles strained to hold on, and then we were back in open sky.

The owl arched her back, tipped her wings, and banked hard to the left. As we turned I could see the full length of a majestic waterfall cascading into a misty granite canyon. My muscles relaxed as the owl continued in a slow upward spiral, riding the thermal air currents without beating a wing. We climbed higher and higher until I could see the river below us flowing all the way to the ocean.

In the distance to the south I could see a second river winding gently through lush green farmland. As we circled back toward the north a third river came into view. This one more rugged and wild than the first. Each river was unique unto itself and yet their separate paths flowed in the same direction. The rivers did not struggle with this journey. They followed the path of least resistance from mountain to sea. The topography of the land created three distinct routes but the life force that flowed through them came from and returned to a common source.

As we circled higher still, I could see and feel the unity and the diversity of the three rivers. They were united by their commonality as much as they were defined by their uniqueness. The higher we climbed the easier it was to see the connection between the rivers. Something about this realization caused my body to relax. I nodded my head in a knowing manner and snuggled into the downy softness of the owl's back.

———————————

I woke up to the soft light of early morning streaming through the bedroom window. The dream had been so vivid and the transition so rapid that it took me a moment to orient myself. It was early dawn, Bonnie was sound asleep and the house was quiet. I slipped out of bed, this time with complete ease, grabbed my journal and went looking for a place to write. I wanted to capture the essence of the dream while it was still fresh in my mind.

The combination of the encounter with the owl in the field and the lucidity of the dream put me in a reflective state. It was easy to get my thoughts down on paper. Bonnie and her housemates started to stir. I closed my journal, made a pot of coffee, and put on a long sleeve shirt to cover the gauze wrapped around my forearm. I didn't want to explain what had happened during the night. I hung out through the end of breakfast but wasn't engaged with the morning conversation. I excused myself, told Bonnie that I would call her later, and headed for Eld Inlet to collect my thoughts.

Over the next few days the memory of the encounter with the owl and the images from my dream stayed with me. The combination of events had started to crack the foundation of my normal waking reality. The more I thought about it, the more I felt like I had journeyed to the edge of another world. I was not able to hold the experience fully, but neither was I able to put it down. It followed me around like a stray dog.

On the twenty-eighth night I walked barefoot on my way to Eld Inlet. I was looking for a way to ground my body and expand my mind in an attempt to understand what I had begun to refer to as *owl medicine*. The whole thing was still a mystery to me and at the same time there had been a healing quality to the experience.

By the time I got to the beach I was more relaxed. I realized that I had been pushing too hard to understand something that simply needed to steep awhile longer. I had been resisting the *not knowing*. The more I had struggled to understand, the more distant the understanding became. It was only as I allowed myself to be in the unknowing that I began to feel whole once again.

As I stood on the beach, I had an image of the afternoon that José Humevo had told me to wade in the water as a way to ground myself. I stepped into the water and immediately felt a sense of relief. It was both soothing and stimulating. I rolled up my pant legs and walked further into the salt water. My body wanted more.

I returned to the beach, took off my clothes, and waded back in. I stopped when the coolness of the water touched my genitals. I took a breath, told myself to relax, and continued. I stopped again when I got to my waist, but this time it wasn't resistance to the cold water that stopped me. It was the magic of the moment.

The air was still, the water perfectly calm, the sky crystal clear. I looked at the surface of the water and could see the reflection of the stars above me. The effect created the illusion that I was completely surrounded by stars. Stars above, stars below. I was floating in the middle of the cosmos and could feel a greater presence hovering all around me. I nodded my head to acknowledge the end of my twenty-eight day practice and said a quiet thank you to *All That Is.*

THE ONLY DANCE THERE IS

◆

I HAD NOT fully understood or appreciated the pauses between the moon cycles when José Humevo first introduced the concept to me. As it turns out, the duration from new moon to new moon shifts from cycle to cycle. It vacillates between twenty-nine and thirty days. José Humevo had settled on a twenty-eight day practice because it closely matched the various cycles of the moon while providing a short resting point between one cycle and the next. It was the space created for *not doing.*

I finally had a couple of nights free and Bonnie and I drove to Seattle for a change of scenery. At some point during our weekend outing she noticed the cuts on my arm and wanted to know what had happened. I told her the story of my encounter with the Great Horned Owl and the ensuing dream. Bonnie was fascinated with the story but couldn't understand why I hadn't shared it with her earlier.

"I didn't want to talk about it in front of your housemates. I was still feeling disoriented from the experience."

"Why didn't you pull me aside and tell me in private? I thought we had agreed to be open with one another."

"We did agree and I am being open. I am sharing with you now. I was trying to understand the experience myself. The whole thing is still not all that clear to me."

"Well it's certainly clear to me, the owl is your totem animal."

"I don't know..."

"What's not to know? How many people do you know who have been cut by the talons of an owl in the middle of the night, immediately followed by a vivid dream about flying on the back of an owl?"

"Uh...none."

Bonnie flashed a look of smugness in my direction. I didn't have a comeback. Our weekend in the city was not unlike the rest of our relationship – kind of good, kind of bad. There were moments of great joy and laughter and there were moments of tension and silence. It was not uncommon for one or the other of us to feel misunderstood and pull inward. And at the same time there continued to be an attraction that brought us back together again and again. The rocky nature of our relationship softened over time but there were never long stretches of uninterrupted smooth sailing.

We both needed some time apart. I dropped Bonnie off at her house, drove to campus, and hiked the trail to Eld Inlet. I found a spot on the beach, hunkered down with my journal, and wrote until dusk. The sky was cloudy so I couldn't see if the new moon was visible or not. I listened to the sound of the waves rolling onto the beach and thought about my experience with the water and the stars. As I relived that moment, the next twenty-eight day practice popped into my awareness. I smiled to myself and headed for home.

I returned to the beach early the next morning, took off my clothes, and waded into the chilly waters of Southern Puget Sound. I was going to train myself to be more conscious about my patterns of Embracing, Allowing, or Resisting. The water would be my teacher.

At some point during my childhood I had adopted a pattern of how to get myself into cold water. I would wade in to about mid thigh, stop, and assess the situation. This became my go/no go choice point. I would either dive in headfirst or abort the mission and return to the beach. Sometimes this decision took longer than other times, but the outcome was always the same, headfirst into the water or back to the beach.

The other night I realized that it had been my resistance to slowly immersing my balls in cold water that had created this pattern in the first place. It was not an altogether unreasonable response. I understood from my night hiking experience that resistance in one area of my life had a tendency to seep into other areas – usually somewhat unconsciously.

150

I was aware that my unconscious patterns, beliefs, and assumptions were dictating the direction of my life. Bonnie was a prime example of this. She activated my patterns, beliefs, and assumptions all the time, the good as well as the bad.

My intention was to highlight these unconscious responses, to help me recognize and alter the way they affected my choices. The idea was to walk into the water one step at a time while remaining relaxed. The practice was to Embrace the cold water as it moved further and further up my body, to welcome it, to enjoy the experience. If I wasn't able to Embrace the sensation of the cold water, then I would attempt to Allow it, to accept it in a neutral manner without a positive or negative association.

If I found myself tensing up, I would stop moving forward, tug on my ear as a way to acknowledge that I was Resisting, and then consciously choose to Embrace or Allow the experience. If I could not move beyond the Resistance then that would be as far as I would go. The goal was to reprogram my unconscious patterns, to learn how to recognize when those patterns of Resistance showed up and to see if I could move beyond them.

I stepped into the water with my awareness and intention firmly in place. Doing the practice turned out to be a bit more demanding than thinking about doing the practice. I couldn't get beyond my belly button that first morning but I knew that I had plenty of opportunities to improve in the days ahead.

My reaction to the water changed dramatically from day to day. Some days it was relatively easy for me to completely immerse myself, head and all. Other days it was a challenge to get past my waist. Over time I learned how to relax, to Embrace and Allow that which I used to habitually Resist.

I enjoyed going to the beach early in the morning; the cold water woke me up and kept me alert all day long. Typically, I would walk into the water as far as I could, return to shore, dry off, and enjoy a cup of tea from my thermos. Sometimes I would write in my journal. Sometimes I would sit quietly and savor the solitude.

One morning near the middle of the twenty-eight day cycle I walked slowly into the water with relative ease. I only had to stop a couple of times to remind myself to relax. I got up to my neck and then slowly bent my knees to fully immerse my head. I had discovered that at a certain point my body became too buoyant to keep walking forward. Bending my knees was my way of completing the gradual immersion.

My head went under the water, cutting off the sound of the seagulls and the waves. When I came up for air I heard a strange sound behind me. It was... applause. I turned to see José Humevo standing on the beach, smiling and clapping his hands.

"Buenos dias," he yelled in my direction.

I returned the greeting and made my way back to shore. My immediate impulse was to give him a hug as we came face to face. As I reached out to embrace him he held up his hands and opened his eyes in an exaggerated manner. I looked down at my naked body dripping with water. José Humevo stepped back in mock revulsion and stuck out his arm as far away from his body as he could.

"A hand shake will be sufficient this morning." We both laughed. It was good to see him. I grabbed my towel and started to dry off while José Humevo watched me, shaking his head.

"What were you doing out there?" He had an amused look on his face.

"It's my latest twenty-eight day practice."

"I suspected that much, but what is the practice?"

"It's the *ear training*. I'm learning to recognize where I Embrace, where I Allow, and where I Resist."

"Why were you tugging on your ear?"

"How long have you been watching me?"

"For awhile. Answer the question please."

I explained that pulling my ear was a way of reminding myself to relax. He shook his head and kept smiling while I was getting dressed.

"You are more creative than I thought. Your water walking routine seems a little severe but I can certainly see how it would be effective. I would like a detailed account of your actions and observations since we were last together."

We sat down on the beach. I poured a cup of tea and started talking. The information flowed out effortlessly. José Humevo nodded his head up and down as I talked. Occasionally, he would stop me to ask a clarifying question. He laughed out loud many times. When I finished he closed his eyes and sat in silence for about thirty seconds. Then he stood up.

"Let's get some breakfast. The Art Deco, my treat."

"Sounds good to me."

I grabbed my pack and followed José Humevo into the forest. Halfway to campus I heard the sound of wings close to my head, immediately followed by the flash of a pileated woodpecker darting right between us at eye level.

I stopped walking. "Did you see that?"

José Humevo turned and stared at me. "The real question is, did you see it?"

"Of course I saw it, he almost hit my head."

"Nils, you must allow your vision to broaden if you want to see the entire picture."

"What do you mean?"

He just shook his head, chuckled, and continued walking. I started to protest but he cut me off with a wave of his hand. "We have much to do today."

We continued in silence through the forest and across Red Square. The courtyard was completely empty. It was still early in the day. We climbed into my car and drove downtown to the Art Deco. After we ordered our food I asked José Humevo the question that had been gnawing away at me for several weeks.

"Is the Great Horned Owl my totem animal?"

"What do you think?"

"I don't know. I'm not sure I know what a totem animal is, exactly."

"If you are unclear, then the owl is not your totem animal. Finding your totem animal is a personal affair. It is an awareness that you must discover on your own. No one can tell you who or what that animal may be. However, as your guide I can point you in a direction that may be useful. From there it is up to you to find that which you seek.

"A totem animal is an aspect of one's life which is both me and *not me*. It is clearly separate from self and yet it is a part of self at the same time. There is a connection that takes place on a deeper level. Recognizing this deeper connection is accompanied by an undeniable internal alignment.

"Finding your totem animal is an important rite of passage for any human being. It opens a conduit into a world where that which is separate is also connected. When your totem animal appears it is a reminder that another level of awareness is available to you. Totem animal sightings should not be taken lightly. These encounters are a gift from *Ati*. Always pay attention to what you are thinking, feeling, or doing when your totem animal appears. Something is being highlighted. Use this information to move yourself forward. This is all I can tell you. All of this will make more sense as your path unfolds. Remember, understanding follows experience, not the other way around."

"If the owl is not my totem animal, what was the meaning of that encounter?"

"The owl was a messenger."

"A messenger?"

"Yep."

"And what was the message?"

José Humevo looked me in the eye. "You are being lazy."

I stared back at him, not sure how to respond. There was a moment of uncomfortable silence between us. I watched as he reached across the table and hit me between the eyes with the middle finger of his right hand. He flicked his finger at my forehead as if he were shooting a spit wad.

"Quiet your mind and listen to the deeper voice within. The experience is dripping with symbolism."

"I'm sorry, I just don't get it."

Bam-bam-bam. He hit me again. This time much harder. The jolt reverberated down my body. It jarred something lose inside me. It hurt in a place I could not define.

"How many times did I hit you?"

"Three."

"And how many scratches did you receive from the owl?"

"Three."

"How many times did the owl flap his wings? How many times did he blink at you? How many times did he hoot in the night?"

"Three, three, three."

"Three. That's right. And how many rivers were in your dream? Are you beginning to notice a pattern?" He blinked his eyes three times. "Sometimes the message is so obvious that we gaze right over the top of it in our attempt to understand. What is the message here?"

"Three is an important number?"

"Yes, three is a very important number. Earth, sun, moon; *Ati*, me, *not me*; body, mind, spirit; infinity, eternity, now; Embrace, Allow, Resist; third time's a charm. Three is everywhere."

"But what does it mean?"

"It means that you need to pay attention to all that is three. The message could not be any clearer. You have an uncanny ability to know and not know at the same time. There is something about three that will help you remove the filters from your portals. You are so close and yet so far from opening the doorway to another world."

José Humevo pulled out a pen and drew a triangle on his napkin. "Let's revisit *Ati*."

"There are three primary components to this triangle – *Ati*, me and *not me*. Each component has three additional subsets. *Ati* is the foundation as well as the contents of the entire universe. It is infinity, eternity, and now.

Me is the myriad expressions of *All That Is* experiencing life in unique and individual ways through body, mind, and spirit.

Not me is that with which me interacts. It is the other, the external world that me chooses to Embrace,

Allow, or Resist. Is there any part of this that you do not understand?"

"I understand the basic concept and I am continuing to understand it better."

"Good. Hold that perspective loosely. Your understanding will evolve as your path continues to unfold. There is another way to look at this triangle." José Humevo took the napkin and quickly sketched another diagram.

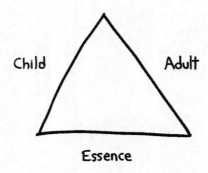

"This is how we start out as human beings. Our essence is connected to *All That Is*. Our child is our experience of me, and our adult is our experience of *not me*. As a child we choose to Embrace, Allow, or Resist all that is adult. As we enter adolescence the lines between child and adult become blurred, which is why it is such a challenging and confusing time for many people. Then, in theory, we cross over to the point where the adult is me and the child is *not me*.

"The mistake that most people make at this point is

to seal the barrier between the child and the adult. The truth is that that barrier continues to be a semi-permeable membrane in healthy adult human beings. Not a soft boundary and not a rigid barrier, but rather somewhere in between. This was part of the message from the owl. Your body and your spirit understood this immediately. What I am doing now is encouraging your mind to join the other two aspects of your me in this understanding. Does this make sense to you?"

"Yes." I nodded my head. José Humevo's words brought clarity to my mind.

"Good," he said as he slid the napkin into my hand. "Keep this as a visual aid. Let's take a walk."

We left the Art Deco and walked up the street to the state capitol grounds. We strolled through the gardens in silence before José Humevo began to speak.

"I am leaving North America this afternoon and there are a few things I want to pass on to you before our paths diverge." My body stiffened. José Humevo laughed and rubbed my chest with the palm of his hand.

"Breath, relax, trust. Neither of us can stay where we are and move forward at the same time. The *principles of learning* are more than lofty ideas to ponder; they are the signposts that keep us on the path. Whenever you are nervous always bring your awareness to your breath. Focusing on the breath brings us into the moment and helps us Discover Now Again. Now is the doorway that leads to infinity and eternity, that connects us to *All That Is* and helps us remember who we really are. We are spiritual beings having a human experience.

"The *learning cycle* is the last concept I want to pass on to you before I leave. The cycle begins with Awareness. Awareness leads to Intention, which leads to Action, which leads to Assessment, which leads back to Awareness. Around and around it goes. This is the *learning cycle*. You intuited this cycle when you chose your current twenty-eight day practice. I would like you to become more conscious of using this learning tool as a way to keep moving forward."

"I'm not sure I understand what you mean. How did I use the *learning cycle*?"

"How did you decide to practice the *ear training* by slowly dipping your body into Puget Sound?"

"I don't know. I just decided."

"Really?" José Humevo arched his eyebrows. There was a moment of silence between us as I tried to make the connection.

"I'm sorry, I don't see how I used the *learning cycle*."

José Humevo raised his hand to the level of my forehead, his finger poised to strike. I jumped backwards and he let out a laugh. "Let me walk you through this. I want to make sure it is firmly anchored in your body, mind, and spirit. The *learning cycle* is Awareness, Intention, Action, and Assessment, in that order. Your Awareness was that habitual resistance had been holding you back. This Awareness came as a result of your solo night hiking experience. Is this correct?"

"Yes."

"This Awareness led to your Intention to reprogram

160

this habitual resistance by slowly immersing your body in cold water." José Humevo laughed again.

"Go on."

"You didn't stop with your Intention. You followed this Intention with Action. You walked into the water and practiced learning how to Embrace or Allow that which you used to Resist. You did the thing that you said you were going to do. This is a critical step in the process, one that many people fail to understand. Intention and Action work best when they walk hand in hand. Intention without Action is little more than dreaming. Action without Intention can often be a nightmare.

"However, of equal importance is the step which you have yet to take, which is Assessment. How did you do? Did you get the results you were looking for? What did you learn from the experience? The answers to these questions will lead to a new Awareness, which will lead to a new Intention, which will lead to a new Action, which will lead to a new Assessment. The *learning cycle* goes around and around and carries us down the path of human evolution.

"All of life is in motion, held together by cycles and patterns that constantly ebb and flow. When I learn how to balance the overlapping cycles of my life, then I am able to ride the evolutionary wave that is flowing through the individual and unique *pattern of being* that I call me. This individual pattern is defined, supported, and challenged by an infinite number of patterns that I call *not me*.

"Every me is a *not me* for every other me it encounters. This complex web of cycles and patterns works best

161

when each individual me comes into alignment with the natural impulses of deep inner knowing. Coming into alignment with this evolutionary impulse is to discover Advanced Human Awareness. It is the *aha!* moment that changes your life forever. This is the place to look for the answers that you seek. The answers are all around you. They always have been, they always will be.

"Notice when and why and how you Embrace, Allow, or Resist that which you encounter. Open your intake and outlet portals. Review the *principles of learning*. Find balance in your life. Notice the patterns that you create and know that you can create those patterns any way you choose. There is only this moment right here and right now. Infinity and eternity flow outward from this time and place. Discover Now Again and ride the wave of human evolution as far as you can go. This is the only dance there is."

José Humevo glanced at me with a mischievous look on his face. "Is that music I hear?" I stopped to listen before I realized that it had been a rhetorical question. José Humevo turned to face me. He grabbed my shoulders and held them firmly as he spoke.

"You have everything you need in order to move forward. You have the Awareness and you have the Intention, the question is will you follow through with Action and Assessment? You are the only one who can answer this question. The path you choose is up to you and you alone.

"Phase one of the training is complete. Now it is time for you to practice, to explore, to test your wings. Your diligence with the twenty-eight day practice has created an opening, a crack in time that is available to be used as a leverage point. You are standing in that delicate moment between too soon and too late. This is what you have been preparing for. You are as ready as you will ever be and at the same time you will continue to learn along the way.

"Do not take your cues from how other people react to you. You will lose your way if you do. Take your cues from in here." He put his hand on my chest and looked me in the eye. "My final words of advice are these — have faith in your knowledge, trust your intuition, and keep your ego under control. You will be tested on these again and again."

He smiled and rubbed the top of my head as if I were a little boy heading off for my first day of school. His eyes softened. "It has been my great pleasure to have walked beside you. I know that you will do well."

I looked at him in disbelief. Was he really saying good-bye? As I struggled to grasp what was happening, José Humevo shifted his stance and hit me three times right between the eyes with his rapid-fire finger. I experienced a moment of pain that took my breath away and brought my hands to my forehead in an unconscious reaction before I realized that the pain was not in my head. It hurt in a place that I could not describe. I lowered my hands and looked around. José Humevo was gone.

THE PATH WITHIN

◆

THE INDESCRIBABLE PAIN lingered for a few seconds and then vanished as mysteriously as it had appeared. I spun around to look behind me. There was no one there. The delayed impact of José Humevo's disappearance jolted my body and literally knocked me off balance. I steadied myself on the back of one of the garden benches. My head was spinning as I lowered myself to a sitting position and took a few deep breaths. I held my head in my hands until I began to regain my equilibrium. It felt like I was waking up from a dream.

I looked around. I was sitting on a bench, I was at the state capitol, I had walked there with José Humevo – hadn't I? His smiling face and gentle laughter pulsated in and out of my awareness and then began to fade. My confusion turned to anger as a deep sense of abandonment began to stir. The feeling was about to consume me when the words of Jackson Barnes rushed into my mind. "Do not judge what you do not understand."

I ran back to my car and drove to campus. Jackson's office door was closed. I tracked down the program secretary and told her that I needed to talk with him immediately. She informed me that he had left that morning for Mount Saint Helens and would not be back until Monday.

Jackson was fascinated with mountains. He had a friend from the University of Washington who was monitoring the increasing seismic activity inside the restricted zone of the smoldering volcanic peak. A semi-active volcano in the neighborhood was too much for him to pass up.

I walked to the bench in Red Square; it was the only comfort I could find. As I sat down I realized that I'd forgotten to ask José Humevo about the seventh *principle of learning*. It was so ironic that I had failed to confirm the accuracy of this particular principle. I didn't know whether to laugh or cry. My flexibility was certainly being tested this time.

The thought of being without José Humevo left an empty feeling in my stomach but I knew that I had to keep moving forward without him. That, after all, was the purpose of the training. I replayed his final words over and over in my mind, looking for a clue. José Humevo did not throw words around casually. There was always a point to what he had to say. In what direction was he pointing?

I returned to Eld Inlet the next day to continue my *ear practice* and discovered that I was in major resistance. I wanted to talk with José Humevo. I wanted to talk with

Jackson Barnes. I wanted to talk with somebody. I had so many questions and didn't know where to turn.

The following morning I got up at sunrise and had a more productive experience in the water. I felt refreshed as I returned home and sat down to Sunday morning breakfast with Tammy. We were enjoying our weekly ritual when an explosion in the distance shook the house. We ran outside to see what had happened. Nothing appeared to be out of the ordinary.

Then we saw a massive cloud plume billowing into the morning sky. I turned on the radio and heard the report that Mount Saint Helens had erupted. It was May 18, 1980. My first reaction was excitement, a volcanic eruption sixty miles away. Then my heart froze. Jackson was on that mountain!

Tammy and I drove to campus and joined the crowd of students watching television in the College Activities Building. I spent the rest of the day focused on the unfolding news reports. The images of the eruption were stunning but details about casualties were frustratingly sparse. I was no more enlightened by the time I went to bed that night than I had been immediately after the explosion.

By the end of the week, the reports were in. Fifty-seven people died on the mountain that day. Twenty-one bodies were never recovered. Jackson Barnes' name was on that second list. The snow and ice that had been such an integral part of his life had mixed with fire and ash and taken his life in a very mysterious manner. The entire college was shaken by his death. It rattled me to my core. I had to summon all my internal strength just to continue my practice.

Jackson's memorial service took place on the last day of my twenty-eight day cycle. The irony of this did not escape me. I was not in an embracing mood. The only glimmer of hope I held onto was the possibility of seeing José Humevo. I carefully scanned the crowd. He was not there.

I didn't have the initiative to begin another practice at the beginning of the next new moon. I went into a tailspin that lasted until graduation. Bonnie and I continued to hang out during the final weeks of our time at Evergreen but we were growing more and more distant. I spent graduation night at her house, more out of habit and convenience than connection and passion. In the morning we had an awkward parting.

Bonnie had a part time position with an off Broadway theatre company and left for New York City that afternoon. I was leaving the following day for a summer job with the Forest Service on the Olympic Peninsula. There was no clear ending point to our relationship. It simply unraveled over time.

Tammy and I moved out of our West Side home, which was a difficult parting as well. I had gotten used to our late night talks, our trips to the grocery store, our lazy Sunday morning breakfast routine. I was going to miss her humorous stories, her frank comments, and her solid friendship. Saying good-bye to Bonnie and Tammy on consecutive days was a bit of a one-two punch. I felt hollow inside as I left Olympia and drove to the coast. I cranked up the stereo on the way but it didn't improve my mood.

I turned north out of Aberdeen and followed highway 101 all the way to Forks. I was a day early for reporting to my job as a firefighter at Snider Work Center, so I drove to Third Beach, near La Push, hiked the trail through the windswept coastal forest, and set up camp for the night. Everything changed as soon as I approached the Pacific Ocean. The sight, the sound, and the smell of the crashing waves began to penetrate the dark cloud that I had wrapped around myself.

Third Beach is a long crescent-shaped shoreline with steep cliffs on either end, giant sea stacks jutting out of the foaming surf, and a hundred foot waterfall cascading onto a bed of rocks and the tide pools below. The late afternoon sun was low in the sky and reflected its brightness and warmth off of the three-foot waves rolling onto shore. Long ribbons of kelp floated gracefully in the bay to the west of my campsite and huge pieces of driftwood were scattered randomly along the beach. I walked barefoot in the sand, waded in and out of the surf and played tag with the waves. I grounded myself at Third Beach and reconnected with the part of me that loves to laugh and play.

The evening sky turned brilliant red and a thin crescent moon peeked through the broken clouds to the west. The image resonated deep inside and challenged the part of me that had retreated into self-pity. I gazed at the moon and acknowledged the unfulfilled dreams that I had left in Olympia and made a conscious decision to move forward without them. The image of Swede standing next to a pile of ashes came to mind. I could hear the faint echo of his words. "Perhaps one day you will understand."

The new moon dropped below the horizon and I built a fire at my campsite above the beach. The tide came in, the wind picked up, and the clouds parted in the sky. I could feel the softness of the ground beneath me, the cool breeze on my face, and the warmth and the glow of the fire. I could hear and smell the in-coming tide. As I sat alone in the darkness I was aware that the elements of earth, air, fire, and water were all around me. Each element freely offered its own unique quality and asked nothing in return, other than to be recognized as a fellow traveler on this magical journey called life on planet earth.

I felt my energy returning as I reconnected with the world around me. I sat quietly for a long time, stoking the fire and smiling to myself. I can't remember a time when I felt more content to simply sit and be present to the moment. At some point my eyes grew heavy and I knew that it was time for bed. I crawled inside my sleeping bag and stared out into the cosmos before drifting off to sleep.

I awoke in the morning with a dream fresh in my mind. I had been standing on the beach, looking at the night sky. There were seven large celestial bodies scattered among the stars. They were all about the size of the moon, some bigger, some smaller, all brightly colored. An owl flew over head, circled four times, and disappeared as quickly and silently as it had appeared. I woke up.

There was a message here. What was it? The seven heavenly bodies had to be the seven *principles of learning*. The owl was clearly a messenger, but why had he circled four times? Four times, four and seven, four times seven... and then I knew. My next practice was to focus on the seven *principles of learning*. One principle each day of the week, repeated four weeks in a row. It was a twenty-eight day practice.

One of the last things José Humevo said to me was to review the *principles of learning*. This seemed like a good way to follow his advice. It was also an opportunity to practice the learning cycle. I had the Awareness and the Intention, now it was time for Action, and at the end of the twenty-eight days, Assessment. I went through my notes and found the seven *principles of learning*:

Either I run my fears or my fears run me

•

Humor and humility are stepping stones along the way

•

Mistakes are an integral part of the learning process

•

Fear is the problem, trust is the solution, courage is the way

•

When the student is ready, the teaching appears

•

I cannot stay where I am and move forward at the same time

•

Transition points are where flexibility is tested and revealed

My intention was to focus on one principle each day, meditate on it for ten minutes, and then write down whatever thoughts showed up in the next ten minutes. It was a simple twenty-minute exercise. Somewhere along the way José Humevo had told me that twenty minutes was an appropriate period to practice anything. "Twenty minutes is one third of an hour. It's the mystery of three, going the other direction. This is the reason I had you walk barefoot for twenty minutes a day during your initiation period."

I was learning to trust the wisdom of José Humevo. If he suggested twenty minutes, that was good enough for me. I closed my eyes and began to focus on the first principle: either I run my fears or my fears run me. As I focused on these words I realized that it was time to let go and move on. It wasn't until I released my grip on the sadness, the shock, and the surprise of José Humevo's unexpected departure and Jackson's sudden death that I was able to find the gem hidden deep within.

Life is indeed filled with magic, awe, and mystery – all of it hanging from a rather delicate thread. There are no guarantees about the future, no certainties about tomorrow. There is only this moment unfolding again and again, and an endless opportunity to choose to Embrace, Allow, or Resist whatever that moment happens to bring. Jackson Barnes and José Humevo had punctuated this lesson in a manner that was difficult to ignore. As this realization seeped into my awareness I nodded my head in a gesture of appreciation for the gifts I had received from the gatekeeper and the learning guide.

When I opened my eyes I saw a bird perched on a tree next to my campsite, looking at me with a quizzical expression on his face. It was my totem animal. I knew it the instant our eyes met. José Humevo was right, there was absolutely no doubt about who this was. I cannot explain how I knew, other than to say that I felt it throughout my body, mind, and spirit. It was so obvious that I couldn't understand why I hadn't recognized it before. This was not the first time we had crossed paths.

We peered at one another in the stillness and the softness of the morning light for only an instant and then he disappeared into the forest. In that brief moment I could feel the path within begin to open. José Humevo had guided me to the trailhead and handed me a bag of tools to help me find my way. The rest was up to me.

THE PRINCIPLES OF LEARNING

◆

Either I run my fears or my fears run me

Humor and humility are stepping stones along the way

Mistakes are an integral part of the learning process

*Fear is the problem, trust is the solution,
courage is the way*

When the student is ready, the teaching appears

*I cannot stay where I am and move forward
at the same time*

*Transition points are where flexibility is tested
and revealed*

HIGHPOINT EXPERIENCE

———◆———

Highpoint Experience is a training company dedicated to providing transformational learning experiences for personal and team development. Highpoint utilizes a variety of formats to meet the specific needs of a wide range of clients. The publication of *Another Way to Be* is the latest addition to this expanding format.

To learn more about Highpoint Experience, or to order additional copies of *Another Way to Be*, please visit our web site at **www.highpointexp.com.**